MARK MANNOCK

SILENT VOICE

A NICHOLAS SHARP THRILLER (4)

For Jack and Anisha

Contents

Chapter 1

Snap.

Sanit's eyes burst open like a frightened cat, staring into a darkness that yielded nothing.

Something had woken her.

She glanced at the alarm clock on the table beside her bed... 3 AM. Their borrowed house sat amidst several acres of farmland, the long summer nights usually peaceful. That's why Kamon chose it. Kamon... of course. Sanit stretched her arm and slapped the warm space beside her. Nothing. Her boyfriend must be up. These days he barely made three hours sleep a night, yet it seemed unusual that he'd gotten out of bed. Unusual, but not unheard of. That would have been what disturbed her. She exhaled, not even realizing that she'd been holding her breath.

"Shhh."

The tension flooded back as Sanit peered through the blackness to make out a dim shadow in the doorway.

"Not a word. Get up... quickly."

1

Kamon's whispered voice reassured her, but the intensity of his tone was disturbing.

"Now."

Sanit swung her legs out of bed, stood up and reached towards the robe hanging on the wardrobe door. Fumbling in the dark, she pulled the garment tight around her, covering her nakedness.

Without warning, the window shattered, sending clusters of glass shards across the room. Sanit heard nothing except the crack of the gunshot.

"Get down," Kamon yelled. No need to whisper now. Sanit threw herself down onto the bare floorboards. A second later, Kamon's body landed on top of her. Was he hurt?

"Stay low." Aware of Kamon's muscular arms encompassing her torso, Sanit felt herself being dragged through the doorway.

"They've found us," she gasped, slightly surprised at the effort it took to push the words out.

"Yes… again. We've got away before, we'll get away now. Just do what I say."

Reassured by Kamon's confidence, Sanit knew she would follow this man anywhere. He would find a way out.

"When I tell you, sprint for the back door. Don't go through it, wait there for me, and for God's sake, stay low."

"Wait for you? Where will you be?"

Sanit's newfound optimism evaporated.

"I'm going to make them think we're making for the car. Hopefully, the engine starting will distract their attention long enough to give us a chance."

"Let's stay together," Sanit pleaded. "We always stay together."

"I'll be two minutes… at most. Don't worry. We'll be away before you know it."

Sanit nodded, then as instructed, bolted toward the back door. Halfway down the corridor, a staccato burst of automatic gunfire echoed through the house. Wood shredded and splintered in all directions. A stab of pain ripped through her cheek. She raised a hand, touching the moist blood where the small wooden arrows had pierced her skin. Once again, Sanit dived for the floor. She heard a scream. A male.

"Kamon," she yelled as she rolled over. "Kamon."

Nothing.

Sanit felt her world spinning. Less than three minutes ago she'd been sound asleep and safe. Only she hadn't been safe at all.

"Kamon!" She sensed the power of desperation in her own voice.

Still nothing.

Sanit clambered to her feet, but stayed hunched over in an awkward lope. Another smattering of gunfire reminded her of the need for stealth. She swung around and headed back up the corridor before turning right into the lounge room.

Moonlight flooded through the spaces where only seconds ago a row of glass windows stood untouched. The bullets had shredded the furniture, upending some lighter chairs. Across the wreckage, Sanit saw her boyfriend's lithe figure disappear through the window nearest the driveway.

"Kamon, come back. You'll be killed."

The figure vanished silently into the darkness.

Sanit edged her way across the room, avoiding the shafts of moonlight that lit the space like searchlights from a guard tower. She crouched below the bottom edges of the window frames, passing nimbly through the shadows, ignoring the broken glass that cut into her bare feet. Reaching the casement that Kamon used to escape, she raised her head and risked a brief glance. To her relief, she heard no gunfire. She could see Kamon's outline as he headed toward the car. Her boyfriend limped across the driveway, favoring his left leg, his hand pressed down on his right. The moonlight revealed a glimmer of opaque liquid flowing down his thigh, blood.

Sanit let out a whimper before catching herself. Kamon had almost reached their aging Hyundai. No one appeared out of the blackness. No running steps, no one shooting. Sanit sensed the relief inundating her body. Of course, Kamon had been right. They'd expected that he and Sanit would escape through the front door, or perhaps even the back. He always thought ahead of the game. They would make it. But if that was the plan, why did Kamon want her at the back door? Out of the corner of her eye, Sanit thought she noticed a movement in the field. She peered into the night, seeing nothing as a passing cloud obliterated the moon's illumination. She turned her eyes back toward the car. Kamon's hand stretched for the door handle. Maybe they really should escape this way.

Another flash of motion appeared to her left. This time Sanit's stare remained fixed. Was it just her imagination? Her nerves drew as taut as a hangman's rope, but she needed to make sure. No large trees or bushes surrounded the house to provide shelter for any intruder. But what about the ruong - the rice fields with gullies and banks? Could someone hide there? Would a gun work if it got wet? Sanit didn't think so.

She was wrong.

As the three-quarter moon revealed itself again, the land-scape lit up as though somebody had flicked a switch. Once

4

more Sanit gasped, as three black figures appeared from a gully beside the drive. They all held automatic weapons.

"Kamon, run, please run!"

As the cry left her lips, Sanit realized the hopelessness of the situation. Kamon looked around, mistakenly gazing toward Sanit's alarm rather than toward the padi. Sanit started to yell another warning, but her words turned into a scream as the three men opened fire. The barrage of bullets lifted Kamon's body clear off the ground and flung him mid-air against the Hyundai, landing on the vehicle's hood in a splayed, bloody mess. Sanit screamed again. Anguish as a soundtrack.

It took the armed men less than two seconds to assess the situation. After one more burst of gunfire in Kamon's direction, they pointed their weapons toward the house, directly at Sanit's window. Despite her grief, Sanit knew what she had to do. Without bothering to stay low, she scurried across the lounge room and back down the corridor. If the shooting was bad before, it heralded a chaotic level of hell now. Tears streaming down her bloodied face, Sanit scampered the length of the corridor and out through the back door.

At that moment, she expected to die.

After pausing for a split second, surprised that the cacophony of gunfire remained to the rear, rather than assaulting her front on, Sanit ran. Blessed by an erratic moon that slid behind yet another cloud, Sanit ran for all her life was worth. She crossed the yard and dived into the nearest ruong, tumbling badly before finding her feet. She took off down the gully with a desperate energy that astounded even herself. Each moment she expected a hail of lead to perforate her near naked body.

As she disappeared into the blackness, water from the

ruong splashing aimlessly at her ankles, her labored breathing overshadowed the voices and gunfire retreating into the distance. Second by second, it dawned on Sanit that this had been Kamon's plan all along. He knew she would escape alone.

Even in death, he'd saved her.

Chapter 2

LOS ANGELES

Only two things can happen when you stop living your life within the regimented structures of the military. You either search for a framework to replace what you've lost, or you rebel and embrace the chaos of freedom. I thought I'd fall into the former category— a prisoner of routine.

Apparently not.

At this moment, I struggled with one particular set of rules, the California Highway Code… the speed limit. The V12 engine of my late eighties silver Jaguar XJS purred as I accelerated. The more I pressed my foot onto the gas pedal, the more the vehicle responded with the eagerness of a predatory cat. The vehicle remained an indulgence, the speed limit a frustration. After wrestling briefly with the morality of the situation, I allowed the car to surge forward. Rules be damned.

No excuse, no emergency, not even running late, just enjoying myself.

Still, I kept an eye on the rear-view mirror. The Highway Patrol had a habit of appearing out of thin air.

An hour earlier, I'd completed a recording session at a studio down at Long Beach, working with talented musicians and being paid appropriately for my efforts. As I wove in and out of the big rigs that dominated the 710 Interstate, I reflected on my good fortune. After leaving the Marines, I'd found a second lease on life as a professional musician. I now worked in an industry that, if not entirely free, maintained a healthy disrespect for routine. I'd done pretty well, and pretty well had been my aim. There'd been some interruptions along the road. The past has a way of clawing you back.

Sometimes it's better not to dwell.

Contemplating my fastest route, perhaps a quick cut down through University Park toward my apartment at Venice, the sound of John Fogerty's Rattlesnake Highway blared through the Jag's speakers. Wayne De Soto was my manager, Rattlesnake was his ringtone. Someone once said to me that a manager in the music industry needs to be part 'snake in the grass'. I guess Wayne was *my* snake, but also a good friend.

"Wayne."

"Nick, how'd the session go?" he asked.

"Easy as, great players, a decent producer and not bad songs."

"You got any gas left in the tank?"

The question had nothing to do with fuel. Wayne would have me working twenty-four-hour shifts if I didn't say no sometimes. I cut him off before he began his sell.

"Actually, I'm beat. An evening with a couple of good scotches and maybe an eighties James Bond movie will fix me." Bring on the retro mood.

"Well, Roger Moore can wait," he responded.

"Not Moore, Timothy Dalton," I replied.

"Either way, I've got a job you won't be able to say no to."

"No."

"Hear me out."

"No." I shouldn't have laughed as I spoke. Give him an inch...

"There's a new band in town. A kind of alternative acoustic mob."

"This is LA, there's always a new band in town."

"Yeah sure, but this lot are different."

"Different how?" Damn. I regretted asking as soon as the words escaped my mouth.

"Purpose."

I'd watched my manager hook so many other people into his ways, yet, I still nibbled at the bait.

"What purpose."

"These guys are some sort of exiles. I'm not sure from where, but they've built a reputation for integrity. They don't sing lame love songs."

"There's nothing wrong with lame love songs, just bad lame love songs." I tried to distract him from pulling me in any further. I wanted to head home.

"I've sent you one of their tunes. Do me a favor and give it a listen."

That seemed to be the easiest plan to get him to back off. "Sure, will do."

I hung up and pressed the link he'd dropped me. Half-way through the second chorus, I stopped the music and dialed Wayne's number.

"What time and where?"

My mistake, I'd have been better off listening to Rattlesnake Highway.

Chapter 3

I turned off Venice Boulevard, slipped down a couple of empty side streets, and drove cautiously along the laneway that backed onto Platinum Sound Studios. After parking the Jag next to the loading bay, out of the way of any equipment vans, I headed up the stairs and through the back door.

The amazing thing about recording studios is that from the exterior, they mostly look drab and factory like. An onlooker would be forgiven for thinking this building functioned as a fruit and vegetable warehouse. Once you entered the facility, that impression changed instantly. Plush carpet rolled underfoot, while natural wood paneling lined the walls. By design, the only sound you heard emanated from each studio, not the outside world.

I wandered down the long corridor past several double thickness soundproof doors, to the main reception area at the front of the building. An attractive woman, early thirties with dyed red hair, a modern style bob and a smile as welcoming as a sunny day, greeted me.

"Nick, hi. Mac told me you were coming."

"Hello Anita, my love. When are you going to leave that aging rascal and be seduced by my boundless riches?"

Nicholas Sharp… smooth.

"Nick, you're a musician. You can't be trusted. Besides, just how boundless are those riches?"

"Okay, you've got me." I shrugged my shoulders, mock deflation.

"They're down in Studio Two," Anita offered me a sly grin. "I think you're going to enjoy yourself."

I retreated down the corridor and pushed open the heavy door marked with a large golden '2'. As I shoved my way through a second door, I stopped in my tracks. A haunting, almost beguiling sound spilled into the air. It expelled an untamed beauty, laced with a bucket load of angst; a momentary insight into the depth of the human spirit. The backing music sounded fine, but the voice drew me in like a hypnotic cobra.

"Nicholas." The crumbly dry voice of Mac Silverman, world's greatest sound engineer, meandered caustically through the air as the music stopped. I looked around. Two young men with long, dark, carefully disheveled hair, lounged on the couch at the rear of the room. Another man, he could have passed for a brother of the first two, stood between the speakers in front of the enormous mixing desk. He looked up at me briefly before turning back to Mac.

"I think she's got one more in her," he said.

"That take sounded pretty damn good," replied Mac, his 'stuck in the seventies' mustache curling as he spoke. "Anyway, let me introduce you to your piano player. Nicholas Sharp, this is Dusit Salae."

As we shook hands over the top of the console, Mac turned to the men on the couch.

"Also… Ram Chanthora and Sonitha Saetang."

Both men stood up. "Call me Sonny," said the shorter of the

11

two.

I placed them as being of Asian heritage, but I struggled to pick from precisely where.

The man in front of the sound desk, Dusit, took charge.

"Nicholas, we need to add piano to four songs. I have an approach and an arrangement in mind for each of them…."

"Dusit," interrupted a low and breathy female voice, "why don't you let Nicholas listen to each song first? Mac tells us he's played on a zillion recordings. I'd like to hear his ideas."

My eyes searched for the owner of the sultry tones. A young woman, late twenties, straight, jet black hair, creamy off-white skin and a disarming smile strolled in from the studio. She skirted her way around the desk and offered me her hand.

"I'm Sanit Mali, the band's singer and lyricist."

Her grip was firm, without hesitation. I looked into her brown eyes. Dusky, complicated. Then again, I'd got into trouble staring at the wrong girl's eyes before.

"I didn't understand the lyrics as I walked in, but your voice has a powerful quality," I said.

Sanit smiled.

Dusit looked up. His wrinkled brow suggested mild annoyance. A control freak. Not unusual in a musician, especially a creative one.

"As you say," he said, responding to the girl's suggestion. Perhaps a tiny sulk.

Four hours later, I flopped my head down onto the keyboard, exhausted. I'd found it easy to intertwine my piano style with Sanit's haunting melodies, but it took a lot of energy. Sometimes she sang in her native tongue, sometimes in English. The takeaway was that the band's music sent a heartfelt, observant, and strongly political message. Unlike many socially aware bands, their anger didn't hide behind their lyrics; it charged through the sound like an angry bear. I held no doubt they remained pissed off with someone, somewhere. They must have liked my work because I ended up playing on eight tracks.

I got up from the studio's grand piano and sauntered out of the main studio into the control room. The three of them sat huddled together on the coach.

"We'd like you to come back tomorrow and play on some more songs. Would that be possible?" asked Sonny.

I looked at the others. Sanit and Ram gazed at me with that wide-eyed, expectant look. Dusit stared at the ground. Awkward.

Eventually he looked up. "Since we lost Kamon, I have had some trouble relinquishing control. But Sanit is correct, you have brought something new to our story. I would be honored if you would join us tomorrow."

Damn. I was booked solid in rehearsals for an upcoming tour.

"Of course I will," I replied. Wayne would have to employ his charm to rearrange things.

Because we planned on coming back the next day, packing up didn't take long. Sonny and Ram left first. I stayed behind to have a chat with Mac, Dusit and the beguiling Sanit. I wanted to learn more about their 'story', and being a victim of my own curiosity, I wanted to hear more about this Kamon fellow.

"We'll see you back at the apartment," said Sanit as the others went. Everyone seemed in a good mood.

As it turned out, that was about to change.

13

Mid-conversation, I realized I needed to call Wayne to put him to work. I patted down my pockets. I'd left my cell phone in the Jag.

"Back in a sec," I said to no one in particular, and set off down the corridor.

As I shoved the soundproof door at the rear of the building open, I stepped into a war zone.

Sonny lay prone on the ground, blood seeping from his right ear. The dull whimpering sound emanating from his mouth spoke to his increasing pain. A large man, six-foot-something, with a body builder's physique, kicked him repeatedly in the side, like a machine. It took me less than a second to realize Sonny's chances of survival were limited.

"Hey!" I yelled. As if that would do it.

At least the thug tearing into Sonny stopped momentarily, distracted by my call.

Out of the corner of my eye, I saw Ram. Although the band's drummer wreaked of toned muscle and a high level of physical fitness, he was struggling. He stood backed against a wall, trading blows with another man. A huge guy. The punches were of the kind that could stop a truck.

I turned my attention back to Sonny. His assailant had resumed the onslaught. The kicks seemed to have increased in force and urgency. Sonny's cries weakened steadily. Always a bad sign. Clearly, the attacker considered me no threat. Just another feeble musician.

I sprang off the loading ramp, wrapping my arms around the man's throat as I landed. He stopped kicking and staggered back two steps. His initial reaction was to lean forward in an attempt to throw me over his head and onto the ground. It was a good tactic. It was good because it worked. I hit the concrete with such power the air was forced from my lungs. I'd been pancaked.

This thug showed strength and speed, but he fought like a creature of habit. No sooner had I hit the ground, than he began a new barrage of vicious kicks, this time with me as his target. One good thing about being a former Marine was that we're reasonably well trained in close combat. On his third kick, I grabbed the man's ankle and twisted it, as though tightening a wheel nut. Technique versus strength. It could go either way.

My assailant grunted in agony. As he went down, I clambered to my feet. Before I could leap over and shower him with a flurry of furious blows, his legs clamped against my ankles and twisted them like a corkscrew. Technique versus strength and technique. The odds had shifted.

My impromptu plan now turned against me, a violent storm of knuckle and bone rained down on my face. Three punches in, I knew I wouldn't last the distance. This guy landed his blows with maximum force and effect. It wasn't the first time my vision had blurred in a fight, but I feared it may be the last. With each attempt I made to raise an arm in retaliation, my attacker swept it away with one hand while he pounded me with the other.

Each effort I made to defend myself grew weaker than the previous. It was all but over.

Abruptly the rain of violence stopped. My assailant froze, before collapsing onto the concrete beside me. I climbed to my feet, uncertain of what had just happened. My tormentor lay there panting, his eyes spiraling in pain. I saw the cause. Sonny had crawled over to a nearby pile of rubbish, found the round metal base of an old mic stand, and slammed it against the man's head. It must have taken all of his strength, because Sonny collapsed onto the ground, bleeding worse than before.

I took the opportunity to glance across the loading area. Ram stood fast, holding his own with his opponent. Obviously deciding to put an end to the fight, his attacker produced a large sap from inside his jacket. Ram stepped back, but the wall behind him blocked an effective retreat. The thug swung, Ram ducked down, avoiding the worst of the blow. Before the assailant could regroup, Ram hit him under the chin with a powerful uppercut. The sap fell to the ground. Ram retrieved it as his man staggered backward. As Ram raised the weapon, the narrow alleyway filled with a mechanical roar. A motorcycle. I looked up.

Wrong. Two motorcycles.

A pair of riders, clad in black leather, rode side by side toward us. They wore black full-face helmets with darkened visors. I didn't need to guess their favorite color, nor did I need to guess their intentions.

Ram's opponent stepped back as the motorcyclist on the right swung between him and the drummer. Ram's reaction time saved his life as he leaped behind an industrial bin. The second rider headed straight toward me. I stood between him and Sonny, bracing myself and readying to yank him from his bike. The plan fell apart when he suddenly veered left before flipping sharply right, his rear wheel skidding wildly as he knocked me to the ground.

The next five seconds changed everything. The second rider, the one who felled me, stopped. Now positioned between Sonny and me, he reached into his jacket and pulled out a Mini Draco AK-47 semi-automatic pistol.

I jumped up and leaped forward. Too little, too late. The

biker fired two clean shots directly into Sonny's forehead, before flicking his bike around to face me. With lightning speed, the gun in his hand suddenly pointed at my chest. The safe shot. We faced off for a couple of seconds. I prepared for the worst. Not that I had a choice. The rider shook his head, revved his engine, dropped the gun back into his jacket and swept past me. His partner maneuvered beside him as they both exited the alley in a blaze of exhaust fumes and noisy engines. Both the original assailants had taken the opportunity to use the bikes as a distraction, climbing to their feet and following their colleagues down the laneway.

I looked over towards the bin, relieved when Ram's head appeared around the corner. He seemed like a tough guy, but in the dim light, I could see the crunched lines on his face. Fear is harder to hide than most people think.

I turned back to Sonny's lifeless body. Ram must have seen it too. His anguished cry swelled from the depth of his soul.

Less than four minutes after I'd walked through the studio's rear door, it was all over.

What the hell had happened here?

Chapter 4

Sanit's body trembled as waves of emotion crashed against her soul. The tears had stopped for now, but the depth of her grief was obvious. We all sat, spread across the couch and floor in the small Studio Two control room. Detective Michael Alroy from the Culver City Police Department's Investigation Bureau had stepped out to take a call. His questions had been relentless and mainly focused on Ram and me. We'd been questioned separately and then together.

"I sense I'm not being told everything," he'd announced before leaving the room, displeased.

I wasn't happy either, I'd had no information to give him apart from how the fight went down. If Ram or the others knew any more, they weren't saying.

"*Is* the detective being told everything?" I asked Sanit.

The singer sat doubled over, sitting on the floor, leaning against the wall below one of the large speakers. Ram was back on the couch, holding his head in his hands. Dusit paced back and forth behind the smaller monitors attached to the mixing desk. Three faces of shock.

"I can't believe Sonny has gone," whispered Sanit. "We've been through so much, for so long. It doesn't seem conceivable." Tears welled in her eyes as she spoke.

Dusit stopped pacing and looked up. "Since losing Kamon, we're sadly aware anything is possible," he announced to the room, "and I don't mean that in a good way." He stared directly at Sanit as he finished speaking.

"You're holding out," I said. "Detective Alroy is right."

Sanit looked around the control room, her eyes probing her friends for guidance. "Perhaps it's time we told the police everything. This is America, they will protect us."

Dusit spoke, his tone low and forceful. "This may be America, but we are merely visitors. If we cause trouble, they'll send us back. We can all be certain what that means."

To say I was confused would be an understatement. Intrigued; possibly, frustrated; certainly. Sonny's death was a tragedy, but my butt had also been in the firing line, and nobody had explained why. That made me curious, and I knew from experience that piquing my curiosity never seemed to end well.

The door opened; Detective Alroy strode back into the room. He looked like you'd imagine a detective would look. Hawkish nose, thinning hair wrestling from black to gray, swept back over his scalp.

"That's all for now, unless there's something you wish to add?" The police officer searched our faces. His furrowed brow and pursed lips showed no sign of expectation. Predictably, no one spoke. "I didn't think so." He offered a tired sigh. "You can be certain we'll need to speak again. At this point, I will record the incident as a mugging gone tragically wrong."

I was looking at Sanit. Her mouth opened, yet she struggled to make a sound. "Mugging?"

"Unless you can tell me something different?" This time

the Detective looked slightly hopeful, his eyebrows raised. Eventually, subdued by Sanit's silence, his face relaxed into a distant despair, hope evaporated.

I'd figured out what Alroy was trying to do but remained mute.

"Apart from Mr. Sharp, you've all given your address as a small apartment off Hollywood Boulevard. Are you all staying there?"

"Yes," replied Ram.

Alroy raised an eyebrow. "Don't stray too far." The detective turned to me. "Mr. Sharp, we'll be talking."

Lovely idea, but I had nothing to tell him.

The studio door slammed closed and once again, I was alone with my new 'friends'.

"So?" I questioned, allowing a slight aggravation into my voice.

"Nicholas, we're sorry we dragged you into this. You should leave. Don't worry about playing on any more songs. Please go. It's for the best." Dusit spoke with a commanding authority.

"I'm not the police, I pose no threat to you, but I believe I deserve an explanation. So, let's hear it."

Nicholas Sharp, stubborn and frustrated.

Silence.

Suddenly a desolate wail shattered the awkward stillness. The waterfall of tears Sanit held back, gushed forth. It took her several minutes to rebuild her composure.

"Two of us have been lost. How much longer do we have? We must do something." Sanit drew a couple of deep breaths. She looked at Dusit. "I know Nicholas can't assist us, but we do owe him some sort of explanation. Chances are Ram would also be dead if Nicholas hadn't been there." More breaths. "At the very least he can listen, he knows America, maybe he'll have an idea that could help." She collapsed back into the corner, exhausted, but staring her two bandmates down, as if daring them to disagree.

"All right," said Dusit. "I don't see how this will aid us, but as you say, time is running out. We may as well tell the story. Besides, Nicholas may be the one who can persuade you to tone down the political content of your lyrics, for the sake of us all."

Sanit shook her head dismissively.

Ram nodded. A consensus.

Damn my curiosity.

Chapter 5

"The truth, that's our problem Nicholas, we sing about the truth. Not '*my* truth', as people keep talking about these days, *the* truth. We sing about *the* truth."

I must have looked as perplexed as I felt. The pitch of Sanit's voice rose in intensity.

"Sonny is dead. That's *the* truth. Kamon is dead, that is also *the* truth. No matter how you spin it, that truth won't change. It can't be *your* truth that Sonny is still alive. He's not going to walk in the door just because you say it's so." Sanit's grief morphed into fury, but I remained clueless.

Ram took over. "In our country, the truth is what our rulers say it is. If they want the people to believe something, they simply state it is so. We have to accept it, if we don't, there are repercussions.

"What repercussions?" I asked.

"Later," he replied, cutting me off.

"A few years ago, our society appeared to be opening up. We had free elections, the ruling family, our royals, took a back seat. We held hope," said Sanit. "As things progressed, more and more of us started speaking our minds. We demanded action, we sought honesty from our leaders. In our case, we sang to everyone who would listen about the truth, about change, about what we needed to do in order to improve our lives. Like America in the 60s. We kind of aspired to be our country's Bob Dylan, Joan Baez, and Woodie Guthrie rolled into one."

"A wonderful time," Ram interjected. "We stood emboldened. We acted with the people, united. In our own small way, we offered them song, and they gave us courage."

"We felt unstoppable," added Sanit.

"But we weren't." Dusit, the fatalist.

"What happened?" I asked.

"Somewhere in the back corridors of government, the power shifted," Sanit continued. "In public, our leaders said they wished to listen to us. The reality turned out to be different. In truth, they craved our silence. In fact, as events came to pass, they insisted on it. The whole thing was a ploy to expose the activists and deal with them."

Ram took over. "Eventually we woke up to their strategy. Gradually, very gradually, members of our movement would simply disappear. The government feigned investigations, the disappearances ruled as accidents, suicides, whatever kept us quiet."

"The laws began to change, but not in the way we hoped," continued Sanit. "Suddenly it became illegal to speak out against or insult the ruling class. They introduced a mandatory prison term. Three years minimum, up to fifteen years."

"And who established the definition of an insult?" I inquired.

"The courts," replied Dusit, "and they remained under the government's control."

"So, what did you do?"

"We considered running, hiding," said Sanit, "but it seemed cowardly. It was our country too. We resolved to maintain the fight, to sing loudly, clearly. We assumed our popularity would make it too difficult for us to 'disappear'. For a while, the strategy worked."

"Then it didn't," said Ram. "More and more of our close friends vanished. Some had quite high profiles, they also felt protected by their fame. It made no difference. The fake investigations continued. Sometimes the authorities even tracked down perpetrators and publicly found them guilty of murder. Sacrificial lambs."

"One night, everything changed," continued Sanit. "We had a close friend who worked for the authorities, he told us there was a list, a government *hit* list, and our names were on it. The worst part was that at least six of the names on the list had already disappeared."

"We had no choice," said Dusit. "We did what we had to do. We ran... for our lives."

"We spent some time in Vietnam. Despite its checkered history, Vietnam is a country that welcomes interaction with the west. At last, we were out of the jurisdiction of our country's secret police. They had no legal power that reached across borders," continued Sanit.

"Sadly, we underestimated our government's reach," added Ram. "Our rulers didn't require 'legal' power to pursue their agenda."

Like the fool that I was, I let myself be drawn into the story. "What do you mean they didn't require legal power?"

Sanit stared up at me. Somewhere deep in her eyes, anger and grief seemed to fight for control.

"Two of our closest friends, they were journalists as well as followers of our music, went missing. They'd fled to Vietnam with us, to continue their work. They published newspaper articles when they could, they started a blog and were very active on social media. Then suddenly they vanished. We searched everywhere, asked everyone, but they disappeared without a trace."

"Sickened with worry, we continued to write and perform. We had to, not only to be heard, but also to protect ourselves," said Ram.

"Then things got even weirder," added Sanit. "I suspected I was being followed, but whenever I looked around, no one was there. I thought I was losing it, but then the same thing began happening online. Comments made on our sites, our movements constantly mentioned and questioned. We were already nervous, but then it became quite frightening. We just didn't know what to do."

"Eventually our two friends were found." Ram looked down at the carpeted floor as he spoke. "Their bodies had washed up on the banks of the Mekong River. They'd stuffed their stomachs with concrete in an attempt to weigh them down."

Sanit sobbed. "These were good people, who fought self-lessly for others' rights to a better life. We were devastated."

Ram cleared his throat, "Sanit and Kamon wanted to stay. They wished to continue the fight from Vietnam. Sonny and Dusit saw my point of view. We argued but agreed to meet the following week to resolve the situation.

"Who is Kamon?" I asked.

Sanit shifted uncomfortably on the floor before catching my eye. "It was during that week they launched an attack on the farmhouse where Kamon and I stayed." She closed her eyes but continued talking. "You must understand, Kamon was more than a band member. He was my lover and my song-writing partner. The night before we were due to make our decision, they gunned him down, murdered. I escaped because he gave his life for mine. The work I do, I now do for both of us. I won't stop."

"Perhaps now?" said Dusit.

"No, not now, not ever." Sanit folded her arms beneath her hunched shoulders. Defiant.

Dusit's gaze fell to the ground. He shook his head as a half-smile appeared on his lips. An affectionate acceptance of defeat. I wondered if there was more to the relationship between these two, at least from Dusit's side.

"Several days later we met," added Ram. "Sanit, in her grief, reconciled to our reasoning. If we were dead or missing, we couldn't help anyone. We fled to the US, coming here to Los Angeles where music is such an important part of your culture. Our music would still be our voice, we'd just have to be heard from a prudent distance," he concluded.

"And, until tonight, we thought we were safe," said Sanit. "It's over now, there is nowhere else to go."

Silence pervaded the room as we sat there. The gravity of Sanit, Ram and Dusit's story weighed on my mind, but these kids needed more than empathy. They needed protection. I couldn't give them that, but I knew someone who could.

I eased over to Sanit and slid down the wall next to her. Suddenly she seemed more like a kid sister who'd come to me for advice. I took her hand. She took a breath so deep I thought she'd suck up all the oxygen in the room.

More silence, the uncomfortable kind.

I reflected over the last couple of years. There had been a few times I'd been able to support people in trouble. Wrong place, wrong time... maybe, but I'd been there when needed.

This one was too big. There's an old American saying, 'you can't fight city hall.' When 'city hall' is a country thousands of miles away, with a list of civil rights issues a mile long, I was powerless. It was also time to be selfish, I still had my own demons to resist, and lately the battle looked to be going their way. Too much time staring at the bottom of an empty glass, not enough effort moving forward. I'd do the right thing here. I'd offer these battled scarred creatives a bucket load of understanding and the advice they sought.

"You need to go to the authorities," I announced. "Sanit is right, this is America, the government can support you. If you run again, these people will catch you again."

I searched their tired faces for a reaction. The downcast eyes, the sagging shoulders and the lack of response told the story. Disappointment. Surely they couldn't have expected more from me.

"I have some friends," I continued, "connected friends. They'll make sure you're put in touch with the right people."

Ram raised his head, Sanit offered a forlorn half-smile.

"Thank you, Nicholas. I know you mean well," responded Dusit, "but it's all right, we'll find our own way."

I pressed my point. "My friends are decent people, they have sway, and they will see you looked after. I promise you."

This time Sanit, Ram, and Dusit explored each other's faces. The pursing of lips, the nod of a head, the sort of silent communication that only worked between lifelong comrades.

"Thank you, Nicholas, we accept. Besides, we have no choice." Sanit smiled as she spoke, but there was no joy in her expression.

"I promise you, it will be all right."

Why the hell did I have to say that?

Chapter 6

My muscles ached so much that climbing the steps to my apartment felt like ascending Everest. After Sanit, Ram and Dusit told their story, the beating I'd taken in the studio alley had receded to the back of my mind. The stairs reformatted my pain, and not in a good way.

The view across my apartment's lounge offered a reassuring vista. Rich white breakers danced through the floor-to-ceiling windows as they crashed onto the beach across the road. My black Yamaha grand piano beckoned in the corner, the therapist in waiting. 'Not tonight', I said to myself. I truly had nothing left in the tank now. A quiet Johnnie Walker Black Label, and a good night's sleep called to me. The idea of the Bond movie had disappeared completely. Who needs Bond when you've had a day like this?

The others had returned to their apartment. I'd offered them to stay with me for a couple of days, but they seemed confident nothing would happen in the next twenty-four hours. I lay in bed staring pensively at the ceiling, restless and sore. The fight in the alley, the images of Sonny's lifeless body lying prone on the roadway, and the confronting trials that Sanit, Ram and Dusit had undergone, played and re-played through my mind. It was like binge-watching Netflix, but with no happy ending.

Not yet anyway, just a lot of unanswered questions. I loathed unanswered questions.

I rose at six and was on the phone by eight, not my normal musician's hours. When I'd told the band I had friends with sway, I referred to one person in particular.

"General, it's Nicholas." Too many calls had started with that simple greeting, belying the trauma that followed. Not this time. Although he'd frequently been supportive, my former Marine commanding officer, General Colin Devlin-Waters was not a man you asked favors of lightly.

"Nicholas, good to hear your voice," came the calming, well-spoken tone. "Just a social call?"

He knew me too well. "No sir, I have a favor to ask." The General was a well-connected man with an unimaginably far-reaching network. He would have government contacts who may help my new musician friends. I told him every detail of the preceding twenty-four hours.

"Sounds as though it was fortunate you were there, Nicholas. I know several people in Homeland Security. More specifically, there are people within Immigration and Customs Enforcement who may be in a position to offer support." Down the line, I sensed the cogs turning over in his mind. "This will fall under ICE's jurisdiction. Can you give me an hour to see what I can do?"

"Certainly sir, and thank you." The General would always be 'sir' to me, never Colin. I hung up the phone.

I took a bath. The warm water placated the pain and stiffness for a while. After some cooked eggs, strong coffee and a small slug of scotch, the world seemed a little brighter.

My cell chirped. The soundtrack to the Charge of the Light Brigade. Another private joke. Funny guy.

29

"Hello again, sir."

"I've got a contact for you, Nicholas. I've already paved the way for your friends to call. They should find empathetic ears to their story."

I took down the number. "Thank you, sir, I owe you."

"You will never owe me anything Nicholas." With that, the line went dead.

Two hours later, I pulled up in front of a jaded-looking apartment block on La Mirada Avenue. I guessed it to be a late fifties, early sixties build. As I climbed out of the car, the traffic from the nearby Hollywood Freeway echoed loudly through the streets. The double-story stucco building stood long and thin, facing onto a cracked concrete car park surrounded by gardens long forgotten. Walkways with rusting wrought-iron railings ran along the front of the building. The tired structure appeared like a setting out of Once Upon a Time in Hollywood. Retro vibe in a budget location.

I traipsed up the stairs and wandered along the walkway until I spotted apartment four, the address Dusit had given me. When Sanit opened the door, her bloodshot red eyes and ashen skin betrayed her state. My own self-pity evaporated.

"Come in Nicholas."

Inside, the apartment looked no better than outside. Neat and clean, furnished in modern, cheap rental furniture. Ram and Dusit sat on a couch, Sanit motioned me to a chair in the corner and then took to a stool beside the small kitchenette.

"I have some news," I announced. The darkness around all their eyes spoke to their weariness, too tired to be excited. "I have a name and a number. It's someone at ICE with the authority to help you. They're expecting your call."

I leaned forward to pass the paper to whoever wanted to take it. Dusit responded. De facto leader.

"Thank you Nicholas," said Sanit. "We appreciate your kindness."

We talked for an hour or so. They told me of their plans to stay in the US, Los Angeles if possible.

"We've postponed the recording," announced Ram. "When this is all over we'll continue, but for now we just need to be safe."

Safe.

"We are not backing down," added Sanit. "We'll make sure people hear our message, both here and at home. It's the reason we've come this far."

Sometimes you can intuitively tell when someone's convictions live deep within their character. These were three such people. I admired them for their courage, and for their resilience.

When I got up to leave, Ram showed me to the door. "Again, thank you Nicholas, we have been fortunate to find a friend like you."

"I'm sorry there's not much more I'm able to do," I responded as I shook his hand, "but I'm certain you can trust the person at the other end of that number."

Promise and trust. Powerful words that should never be misused.

Chapter 7

Venice Beach paraded in front of me, a jostling mess of haze, color and activity. I lay across the lounger on my small first-floor balcony, taking it all in. The joggers, the girls, the bodybuilders and the hustlers. I'd always been more comfortable observing from higher ground, but I liked this much better than lying prone on a rooftop in Iraq. Must have been the girls.

I felt quietly pleased. Although sadly too late to save Sonny, I'd been able to steer his bandmates in the right direction. Nicholas Sharp, doer of good.

Then my cell rang.

"Sharp, what have you done to us?" I immediately recognized Ram's voice. He sounded alarmed, frantic.

"Calm down, Ram, take a breath. Tell me what's wrong."

"You know damn well what's wrong, you sent them after us."

Glued to the phone, I got up, raced inside and scrambled for my car keys. "Ram, what do you mean? What's happened?"

The sound of a car backfiring or a gunshot came echoing through the phone.

"Ram, where are you?"

No answer. I'd made it half-way down the stairs.

"Ram?"

Silence. At best the connection failed, at worst…?

The Jag's V-12 roared as I opened her up, heading toward Hollywood. Cops or no cops, I didn't care, I'd stop for no-one. Twenty minutes later, as the car slewed sideways into La Mirada Avenue, I realized I'd arrived too late.

LAPD black and whites blocked the entrances to the apartment car park, their roof lights flashing red and blue. Uniformed police prowled the grounds. My entrance to the street had been way too dramatic to go unnoticed. By the time I pulled up out front, a Glock 22 pointed through the glass directly at my face.

"Hands on the wheel… now!"

LA cops don't panic easily, but nor are they noted for their patience. I put my hands on the steering wheel.

A towering, well-built African American cop stood next to the car. His hand remained steady, his glare unwavering. He reached down and pulled on the door handle. As he stepped back to open the door, his gun hand didn't falter.

"Out… slowly."

I climbed out of the Jag.

"Officer, what happened?"

"You tell me. You were the one in such a hurry to get here."

"Officer, please…"

A firm hand clasped my shoulder.

"Officer, please call Detective Michael Alroy from the Culver City Police Department's Investigation Bureau. There's more at play here than you may be aware of." I figured if you keep calling a cop 'officer', eventually he'll get the idea you respect him.

"Face on the road now."

"Officer?"

"Now!"

Clearly, the 'officer' approach had failed. I went to ground. "Hands behind your back."

The flex cuffs pulled tight on my wrists as the heat radiated off the blacktop up through my skin. Next thing, a hand that felt like Thor's lifted me backward onto my feet and shoved me against the car. Was it only thirty minutes ago that I sat on a lounger at Venice Beach soaking in the good life?

"Officer, please, Detective Alroy from the Culver City Police, call him."

The cop hesitated for a minute. He looked at me, a quick professional assessment. Then he grunted.

"Explain. You have two minutes before I haul your ass downtown and your fancy car gets towed."

'Haul my ass downtown?' spare me the Mickey Spillane patter. Instead of a sarcastic response, I told the police officer everything about the situation that I could fit into the two allocated minutes. When I'd finished, he said nothing. He just kept looking at me, assessing.

"Dickson, get the sergeant over here," he yelled over my shoulder.

Dickson must have done what he was told, because five long minutes later a uniformed cop with three silver chevrons appeared.

"He's got a story," said my cop.

"Everybody in LA has a story," replied the sergeant. "I'm Sergeant Stone. Talk."

I repeated my tale and again requested they call Alroy.

"Wait," said the sergeant before walking off.

Ten minutes later, he reappeared. In that time, my cop friend

34

and I had grown no closer.

"I spoke to Alroy. Take the cuffs off, he checks out."

Quite pleased with myself for 'checking out', I decided to read a Mickey Spillane book as soon as I could, seeing as how I was living the dream.

"Go through it one more time," instructed Sergeant Stone, my new best friend. I'd told him the story twice already, but in true cop style, he wanted to see if he could trip me up on detail. Every time I'd interrupted myself to ask a question, he ordered me to start again.

After the third telling, I rebelled. "Don't ask me to go through it again. Admittedly, I don't know these people that well, but I've stepped up for them, I deserve some answers."

Stone stared at me with an ambivalent expression. I took his silence as a cue.

"Where are Sanit, Ram and Dusit? Are they all right? Are they safe? Do you have them in custody?

"I give you ten seconds break and you rattle off questions like a Gatling gun." The policeman paused for a moment, before letting out a deep sigh. "All right, I can give you something. We got a call regarding some gunfire and people yelling, quarreling."

"In LA that sort of situation rarely requires this type of response," I replied, waving my arm in the direction of the multitude of uniformed officers.

"It does when the reported gunfire came from automatic weapons," said Stone.

Automatic weapons. What the hell was going on here? "And my friends?" I asked.

Stone tilted his head to one side, raising his eyebrows in

35

a pitying expression, like he was talking to an unfortunate child. "No sign of them. They've smashed the front door of the apartment into a splintered mess. There are multitudes of bullet holes decorating the walls, but no people."

"Blood?" I asked.

"That's the only good news. Our team found some blood on one of the upturned chairs, but not a vast amount."

You know you're having a bad day when bullet holes in the plasterwork and only *some* blood is good news.

"Can I have a look inside?" I expected an unreserved no.

Stone fulfilled my expectations. "No, not a chance," he replied.

"One more question, Sergeant," I said, probably outstaying my tepid welcome. "I assume you're thinking kidnapping?"

"Can't see it any other way. They're internationals, so we've called the Feds. They'll be here shortly."

I nodded, turned, and walked away. I supposed kidnapping was better than murder. There was always a chance Sanit, Ram and Dusit had been kidnapped here, just to be killed later somewhere else, but that didn't add up either. The perpetrators may as well have murdered them right there in the apartment. Too many damn questions and zero answers.

"Sharp," yelled the sergeant. "I've given you some room to move here, but don't push it. We've got your address."

"I know," I replied, "Don't leave town."

Maybe I was getting the hang of the Mickey Spillane thing after all.

Chapter 8

When in doubt... walk. It was a behavior that usually worked for me. One foot in front of the other, let the mind tick over like an idling engine. I walked; the engine ticked, but my thoughts ran to nothing.

I'd been at it for over an hour, walking the Venice boardwalk between city and sea. When I needed the distraction, I searched the faces of street vendors, exercise fanatics, and posers alike. When I required stillness, I turned to gaze across the rolling waves. The sky scrolled above; a passive blue matched by the hue of the Pacific. An hour wasted, and I had nothing to show for it.

The same questions rushed at me relentlessly. Who took Sanit, Ram and Dusit? How did they find them? What happened to them? The answers I sought lurked just out of sight, hidden in the shadows. Out of hand, I dismissed the general's involvement in any duplicitous dealings. My former commanding officer had covered my back too many times in too many situations for me to doubt him. But I wondered, had the great man backed the wrong horse this time? Had he trusted someone he shouldn't? Impossible. General Colin Devlin-Waters was too good a judge of character for that. He remained the most perceptive person I knew when it came to observing the human condition. My three new friends must have been discovered by their pursuers. But why did their pursuers wait until now? They would have had repeated opportunities to take them in far less spectacular circumstances. Perhaps somebody intended sending a message? But to who? What was the point of the message?

More questions, more shadows. Was there anything to gain by going back to the band's apartment? Would I understand more? Maybe. I kept walking.

The heat drained from the day as the sun lost its edge. A good metaphor for my optimism. I checked my cell more often than I cared to count. No messages, no sign, no hope.

Time for a different tack. Medina's, my bar, the place I go when I want to go somewhere, would be opening soon. I changed direction and headed east, away from the foreshore. Medinas.

I'd traveled twenty yards along West Washington Boulevard, when my phone cheeped. A text message. *'Stop at the entrance to the next alleyway. Wait.'* No caller ID. My initial inclination was to ignore the call. On the other hand, curiosity could either kill or satiate this alley-cat. I'd follow the instructions to the corner but would venture no further.

I stood at the end of the laneway for ten minutes, checking my phone, checking out the passers-by. More time wasted. People checked me out. Loitering with intent. I'd give it five more minutes before giving up and moving on. As I thought of Medina's, a dry itch clawed at my throat. Who needed this?

"Nicholas."

I turned so quickly the Flash would've been jealous. There she stood, five foot four, straight black hair and a face that radiated fear... or perhaps something more complex was lurking behind those dark eyes. Her glare burned through me like a laser.

"Sanit. Are you all right? Are you hurt? Where are the others?"

"Walk," she instructed. I walked.

A painful minute transpired before she spoke.

"Why did you and your friend do this to us? Why did you deceive us into trusting you?"

"Sanit, I know you are reluctant to believe me..."

"Don't," she replied, "don't for a second suggest that you had nothing to do with this. The only way we could have been found was through you. We'd taken precautions."

"If you think that, why are you here? And what the hell was that message about waiting by the alley all about?"

"Kamon knew things, clever things. When he met colleagues within our movement that he didn't fully trust, he would arrange a rendezvous, always arriving early to observe. He'd note if they were followed and also read their body language. He sensed qualities in how individuals behaved that I didn't."

"How did I go? Were you able you read me? I asked.

"I'm certain you weren't pursued, but that is all. You look upset and ill at ease, but possibly you are a good actor. Kamon would have known."

"I'm a lousy actor, Sanit. What you see is what you get, except that I'm also bloody angry."

"What gives you the right to be angry?" she asked.

"Because I've been dragged into something I didn't want to be part of, and for some insane reason, I feel responsible for you."

"Guilt perhaps?"

"It sure as hell isn't guilt."

I stared down into Sanit's eyes, her eyebrows slightly raised, hinting at uncertainty. As a military sniper, I'd been trained to read body language too. Many times my life had depended on it. "You've avoided my question. If you don't trust me, why are you here?"

Long pauses, both hers and mine, punctuated the conversation. A minefield of indecision and mistrust.

Finally, she spoke. "Contrary to what logic tells me, I'm having trouble believing I was that wrong about you. Combined with the fact I've lost Ram and Dusit…"

"Lost?"

"We became separated, I have no idea where they are."

Sanit's top lip quivered. Nerves are difficult to hide.

She continued. "Either way, there is no one else I can turn to. You are not my first choice, Nicholas. You are my only choice."

A vote of confidence… kind of.

"If you've made that decision, we need to talk Sanit. Come back to my apartment, tell me what happened, and we'll begin to make a plan."

"I may be lost, a bit frightened and slightly confused… but I'm not stupid. Tomorrow we'll meet in a public place, somewhere I'll be safe. Then I will decide if there is trust."

"We need to talk now," I said.

"Tomorrow."

"Where?" I asked. Stalling for time.

"I'll decide and then text you… tomorrow." The girl appeared agitated, restless, shuffling from foot to foot.

My frustration grew. I had the skills to help this girl, but she required protection now… not tomorrow. I took a few seconds to calm myself, gazing across the street. The early evening's revelers had begun to populate the sidewalks. Joy as a background to pain. All too aware whatever I said now could have a great impact on Sanit's immediate wellbeing, I needed to tread carefully.

I drew a deep breath and turned back to look at her. My calm state had been rendered irrelevant.

Wherever she was going, Sanit had already gone.

Just after midnight, I perched in the shadows across the street from the apartment block. The cops had gone. In the dim light, I noted the yellow LAPD crime scene tape rolled out over the front door. Every fifteen minutes or so a patrol car sauntered past. I'd watched three go by. The cops in the cars had paid scant attention to the building. It would be all about the timing.

I waited until the fourth black and white cruised by before crossing the street and heading up the stairs. I wouldn't need long. They'd covered the doorway with wooden boards, the yellow tape crisscrossing over them.

Los Angeles Police Department

Police Line-Do Not Cross

Taking care not to rip it, I pried the tape away from the boards. The small crowbar I'd hidden under my jacket slipped easily between the wood and what remained of the door jamb. The nails creaked noisily as I worked them loose. Three minutes later, I squeezed through the narrow opening I'd created and stepped into the apartment.

Aware of the possibility that cops in the next patrol car may notice the disruption to the doorway, I needed to be quick. I returned the crowbar to my jacket and pulled out a pocket-sized flashlight. As the beam lit up the space, I realized I didn't need long at all.

The cheap furniture I saw the day before lay shattered beyond recognition. Automatic weapons will do that. No pane of glass remained intact, so the windows had been boarded over as well. The plasterboard walls looked like a target range, the drywall disintegrating through to the wall frames. Over in the far corner, the chair that I had previously sat on had been upended, the remnants of its wooden legs pointing toward the ceiling. On the top of the back of the chair, which was now the bottom, I noticed some evidence of blood splatter across its checkered upholstery. Stone was right, the small amount appeared more likely from a bloody nose than a fatal wound.

The most perplexing aspect was the level of destruction. There was no need to create such chaos in order to kidnap three unarmed musicians. What was the point?

None of this made sense. I certainly couldn't see how the general's contact at ICE would or could have instigated an attack of this nature. Perhaps the foreign authorities chasing Sanit, Ram and Dusit found out where they were staying. That made little sense either, Dusit was certain they'd been safe here. Clearly, they weren't.

I glanced at my watch. The break-in had taken ten minutes all up. Too long. The wrecked state of the apartment and my own questions had distracted me. I slipped back through the doorway, wrapped my jacket around the end of the crowbar before hammering the nails in as quietly as possible. I smoothed the tape back into position before scampering down the stairs and into the darkness across the road.

Less than a minute later, a patrol car rounded the corner at the end of the block. It cruised slowly down the street. I pressed myself further into the shadow of the building that sheltered me. The black and white stopped five yards from my location. The cops inside stared at the building. I saw why. The top strand of yellow police tape had come loose, now flapping in the breeze. There was some discussion between the two cops. I slowed my breathing and held my position, frozen in stillness. Four minutes later, the patrol car accelerated away from the curb.

Mickey would have been proud.

Chapter 9

If I needed to protect someone, I'd take them as far away from the throb of humanity as possible. Somewhere remote, the desert, an island, perhaps the Rockies. Sanit had an alternative concept of how to stay safe.

A throng of bodies, moving to a mystical, unsynchronized rhythm, flooded the Universal City walk. Crowded shops lined the wide space, queues snaking out from each front door. My temper flared when I received the text telling me the location of our meeting. It flared again as I surveyed the mass of people separating me from the studio theme park gates.

I plowed my way through, ignoring the bumps and shoves as tourists jostled for position to spend their money before heading through the turnstiles. Any one of them could have had a gun, or a knife. I'd have no chance to see a weapon in time. This was a stupid idea.

When I made it to the Globe Fountain, our place of rendezvous, I waited. If Sanit did her watching thing again, she'd have no success here. She'd find more luck following a single seagull in a flock of thousands. Thirty minutes later, I was worried. Sweat trickled down my face as I scanned the multitude of faces. Sanit's lack of height didn't help. Twenty minutes after that, my doubt turned to certainty. Something had gone wrong.

"Nicholas."

She'd done it again, appearing out of nowhere.

"Sanit, where the hell have…"

"I am sorry. I didn't intend to keep you waiting. I suspected someone had been following me, but in the end, I saw no one. I am nervous and I think my imagination got the better of me."

It had been my experience that if you sensed somebody was watching you, they probably were. Gut instinct is a reliable source, but I let it go.

"Let's get out of here," I suggested. "This is too big a crowd."

"No, Kamon taught me to seek safety in crowds. We stay here."

Kamon, may he rest in peace, was playing on my nerves. "We must leave Sanit, we must leave now."

She responded by walking away toward the entrance. So much for making a stand. I followed, subservient male to the end.

As I paid for our tickets, I paid little attention to the attendant taking my money. My eyes darted everywhere, searching for any movement that betrayed a threat. Nothing.

"For God's sake," I said. "Can we get a drink? The heat is stifling, even for LA."

Once into the theme park, I turned and headed to a nearby kiosk. My turn for a tantrum. A table with two chairs stood empty, a miracle. For once, Sanit followed. She sat down on a chair. I grabbed a couple of light beers, again focusing on those around me.

"Hey, watch your step buddy!" The southern drawl belonged to an overweight man in a brightly colored Hawaiian shirt. I'd bumped into his protruding stomach. "Get a load of this guy

Stella," he continued, talking to a tight-faced woman with a 60's style bouffant, trying to ignore two squabbling children. Did these people model themselves on the Bundys?

"Sorry," I muttered. My heart raced as I realized he blocked my line of sight to Sanit. I shoved my way around him, spilling the beer as I went.

"Hey."

Enough. I pivoted and gave him the look I'd perfected when interrogating insurgents in Iraq. He shut up and turned around. If looks could kill.

To my relief, Sanit remained in the same position. I set down the two now half-filled glasses on the table in front of her.

"I don't drink alcohol," she said.

"Wonderful."

I took a swig of beer and assessed the girl in front of me. Emotionally she was an enigma. Strong-willed, but frightened, a dangerous combination. Physically, Sanit looked a mess. The black lines around her eyes plus her rag-doll body language spoke to her exhaustion. She'd obviously made some attempt to tidy her hair but hadn't been overly successful. I figured she'd slept rough the night before, or close to it.

"Sanit, you're a wreck. You can't go on like this. We need to make a plan, move forward. I don't want to sound harsh, but unless you've got something else up your sleeve, you require my help to survive." Subtle.

She cast her eyes downward. Unsure whether she'd begun building herself up for another attack on my trustworthiness or a gradual acceptance of defeat, I waited. When she glanced up, the fight had gone.

"I have no choice. I must trust you Nicholas."

At last.

"Okay, you can begin by trusting me when I say we need to leave," I said.

"No, we stay," came her terse reply.

Two steps forward, one step back.

I searched the eternal flow of faces. "All right, let's at least reduce the crowd size and the risk. We'll take the studio tour."

She sighed, then nodded.

We hustled forward through the throng. Sanit paused briefly as we hurried past one attraction, Springfield USA. She peeked around expectantly, before shaking her head.

"Just my silly imagination."

I looked behind as well. Pointless.

A few minutes later, we stood under a bright blue canopy, part of a winding line separated by metal barriers. Everyone seemed excited about the upcoming tour of the magical world of movies. I just wanted to keep moving.

Eventually we boarded one of the chain of open trolleys decorated with the Universal Studios logo. We jostled down to a pair of vacant rear seats. As we sat, Sanit looked around again. I glanced across the crowd too, looking for anyone suspicious. Then I wondered, what does a suspicious person really look like? Maybe I should have asked Mickey Spillane.

As the trolley pulled away, I let out a sigh of relief, Sanit, a sharp gasp. Panic.

"What?" I asked.

"Over there... at the back of the queue... the big guy. I'm sure he's one of the gunmen that came to our apartment."

At the rear of the line of tourists, stood a large, broad-shouldered man. His hair jet black. Even at some distance, his muscular physique bulged through his shirt. The giant looked directly at us. Every couple of seconds he glanced

47

away purposefully, but each time his gaze returned to where we sat.

"Are you sure?" I asked.

"Not completely, but mostly. Nicholas, what do we do?"

"Welcome to the world of movies," Jimmy Fallon, or at least his recorded image, introduced the tour. I ignored both the comedian and his live counterpart standing at the front of the leading trolley.

"Sanit, if you're right, it's a problem. On the plus side, we're pulling away, and he's stuck at the back of the line. That gives us time."

She gazed at me, not teary, just defeated. "Nicholas, these are professional, trained kidnappers, killers. They will not give up. With respect, I'm a singer and you're a piano player. What chance do we have here?"

I wanted to reassure her, but I held no doubt about the depth of trouble we faced. "Sanit, I had a life before becoming a musician." In reality, my past hung over me like a looming shadow. "I think I'll be able to help."

She looked unconvinced but offered a small smile at what she perceived to be my false bravado.

The trolley train rattled on, winding its way down the hill, toward the famed Universal backlot. I'd always enjoyed the sense of cinematic history when I'd brought visitors here. Not today. As we descended along Timeline Drive, movie posters from all eras lined each side of the road, drawing tourists into the Hollywood story.

Nerves on edge, I maintained a constant vigil, eyes scanning the environment. No one appeared to be following, but with security personnel everywhere, how could they?

We passed Fire Station 51, Universal's own functioning

firehouse, before easing onto the flatter ground that held the complex's thirty-five sound stages. We'd entered the real world of fantasy. Universal functioned as a professional studio, so while they had dedicated some sound stages to house 'tourist events' most operated as regular production facilities, working daily.

Sanit sat frozen, staring ahead, her hands clutching the safety rail. Murdered friends and fleeing for her life must have led her into a vortex of fear. Who could blame her?

I rallied my thoughts. It seemed likely the people pursuing Sanit would be waiting for us when the tour finished. In that crowded atmosphere, it would be difficult for me to protect the girl. Only one solution came to mind.

"Sorry, Sanit, you're going to have to forget about seeing the backlot. We're leaving the tour early."

She remained rigid, her eyes moist, but mesmerized by the view before her. I wondered what she saw, certain it wasn't the back of a trolley seat.

"Sanit, listen to me. Now is not the time to freak out." I shoved her gently on the shoulder. She jumped like a scorpion had bitten her.

"What? Yes, sorry Nicholas. What did you say?" She'd returned.

"Get ready to jump, we're out of here."

Our tour guide had just announced the first of the backlot stages, the New York street, when I grabbed Sanit's hand. As those around us swore and cursed, we clambered past a middle-aged couple in the next seat, before climbing through the open space between the side of the trolley and the roof.

"Jump, now!" I yelled.

We heaved ourselves over the edge and onto the hard asphalt

roadway.

Sanit stumbled, but I grasped her hand. "Run, don't look back."

After the shade of the trolley roof, the harsh heat of the LA midday sun blazed down on my skin as I pulled Sanit toward the first building offering shelter. We ran straight down a laneway between two huge soundstages. Wide enough for a couple of vehicles, but not much else. The building's doors appeared locked tight, suggesting the buildings remained unoccupied. We reached the end of the laneway and jogged onto a roadway running crossways. After veering left, we swung hard to the right, finding ourselves behind another soundstage.

It would take a couple of minutes for any message to reach the driver in the front trolley of our group. How he'd react to the news that a pair of runaways had made a break for freedom was anybody's guess. I figured they'd choose not to chase after us; slowing up the chain of tours following would be problematic. They would, of course, ring security. Right now, I felt okay about that. I didn't mind the idea of some good guys with guns coming to our rescue. Our immediate aim was to get far enough away from the tour that they would have to send a decent size team to chase us, but not so far away that they couldn't find us.

The next soundstage loomed above us. In the laneway beside it, cars and vans stood stationary alongside the building. Halfway down, a large open sliding door revealed a place to hide. Beside me, Sanit struggled for breath. Hobbling badly with each step, her right ankle struggled to support her meager weight.

"Sorry Nicholas, I'm slowing you down. I landed badly when

we jumped off the trolley. I don't think anything's broken, but it hurts."

I surveyed the laneway behind and ahead of us. No one followed. I pulled Sanit sideways between two parked vans. It wasn't as secure as the building, but it would do. We crouched down, out of sight... for now.

"Take a break," I announced. "We'll stay here a moment. Security will be along soon enough, and they'll be our safe ticket out."

I was quite pleased with my plan... until I wasn't.

Chapter 10

"Do you have a mirror in your bag?" I asked Sanit.

"Yes, but why?" With a weary sigh, she drew a small square mirror out of her denim carryall and passed it to me.

I positioned the mirror downward, opening the angle to show activity in the laneway without me having to stick my head out. I saw nothing. I flipped myself around to check the other direction. Same result.

"So, we just wait?" asked Sanit.

"Yeah, we wait. I'll keep monitoring the laneway, to be sure. We should be okay as long as nobody moves either of these vans. I peered through each van's windscreen. Parked head-to-head, presumably for easy access to the back doors, they appeared to be tech vehicles of some sort. One contained cables and lighting equipment. The other held tools and some short lengths of wood. Set construction.

After a couple of minutes, I angled the mirror to check the laneway again. All good in the direction we'd been heading in. Again, I flipped over and checked the way we'd come.

He stood there. An enormous man, Asian heritage, head scanning left then right, searching... for us. I yanked the mirror back.

"We've got a problem. There's a guy at the end of the lane.

He's built solid as a barn. I'm thinking he could almost be the twin brother of the man we left in the queue at the trolley station."

Sanit's jaw dropped.

"Hang in there, Sanit, we've got to work through this," I tried to reassure her.

I risked the mirror one more time. He remained there, but a fresh problem reared its head. How the hell did an intruder make their way into a secure facility like Universal, while carrying a Mini Draco AK-47 semi-automatic pistol?

"If that bloke walks in this direction, he's going to see us. We've got to make it to the other end of the laneway." Again, I used the mirror. The thug had pivoted. He stood facing back up the roadway, away from our position. "Come on," I commanded, "let's go."

Sanit gathered herself and stood up. I grabbed her shaking hand and headed for the gap in the buildings. We bolted quickly and quietly, aware the intruder may turn around at any time. I glanced behind me. So far, so good. We'd tracked halfway down the side of the building when a second figure suddenly rounded the corner ahead of us. The man from the trolley terminal. He also carried a Draco.

"Hey," he yelled as he saw us.

He'd got his friend's attention and ours. We'd gone from a slim chance of getting out of this to no chance at all. As the second man raised his weapon to fire, I yelled at Sanit "Stay low, zigzag, and run like hell." If we were destined to die, I wanted to do it with purpose.

Bullets splattered the concrete around our feet as we weaved our path forward. Both men feared firing blindly lest they hit each other. They aimed low, carefully. Our target became the open door half-way along the soundstage wall. Ten yards to go. It was possible. The deluge of firepower caused concrete pellets to stab at our shins, three yards to go. One yard.

"Jump," I screamed.

We tumbled through the doorway before halting abruptly. Another giant stood in our path. My first thought was that the fellow looked vaguely familiar. I figured I may have unwittingly noticed him following us in the crowd. I noted his square jaw and penetrating stare almost as quickly as I noted the gun in the shoulder holster over his shirt. I had to get the gun before he did.

Shoving the man backward with the flat palm of my right hand, I reached forward with my left and grabbed the weapon's handle. It released easily. As I rounded up on my target, I pointed the pistol at his chest. Any moment the other two thugs would come charging through the door. We had a ten-second window of opportunity... at most.

The man reacted unpredictably. A professional. Instead of standing his ground, he leaped backward. Not what I expected. His pupils dilating like saucers, his jaw dropped open. As I stepped forward, he let out a piercing scream before retreating into the darkness.

Then I realized I'd misread the situation. He was a professional... a professional actor.

A noise echoed through the vast space. There was some sort of commotion at the opposite end of the soundstage. Through the shadows, I made out the reflection of bright lights on the other side of some makeshift wall paneling. It looked to be a movie or television set; a place busy with people. Sadly out of reach, it was too far away for us to make the distance before our pursuers caught up.

"Quickly, back to the door," I ordered Sanit.

Three steps later, I pulled her into the semi-darkness beside the open doorway. On cue, the first thug entered the room. He paused at the entrance, surveying the enormous space. He blinked several times as he adjusted to the light. He hadn't noticed us huddled in the shadows.

Once his eyes refocused, he ran on toward the set in the far corner. We waited.

The second man entered the same way. Panting heavily, he'd had the furthest to run. He paused before eyeing his accomplice a third of the way across the room. I had a plan, but it was flimsy as all hell.

I vaulted from the shadows and leaped onto the man's back. I had a fraction of a second to get this right or it would be a bust. Wrapping my left arm around his thick neck, I held my newly acquired gun to the man's temple. He attempted to shake me off, heaving his shoulders back and forth.

"Drop your weapon or you get a bullet in the head." He would have felt my breath in his ear.

The man hesitated briefly, before letting the gun fall to the floor. The weapon clattered onto the concrete, attracting the attention of the first man. He swiveled toward us.

"One step in this direction and your friend dies," I shouted.

The thug in the distance stopped, but he didn't raise his weapon.

This had all the trademarks of a good movie showdown. The first man hesitated, appearing to consider if his colleague was worth saving. The man I held probably wondered if these were his last moments on earth, while I questioned my own ability to pull this ruse off. I remained all too aware that the pistol I held to this thug's head was as fake as the actor I'd taken it from.

I turned to Sanit, "Grab the gun from the floor, please."

Sanit's nerves seemed to have evaporated, replaced by a wave of slow-burning anger. She strode forward and picked up the Draco.

"Over here," I said, trying to sound as casual as possible. If my man sensed fear, he would act.

Sanit marched over, "Shall I cover him?"

From weeping angel to warrior in ten seconds flat.

"No, give the gun to me, please." Calm. Sanit did as asked.

Once I had the Draco in my hand, I felt a little better. Now it was almost an even match.

My eyes remained fixed on the man across the room. He would be aware, as was I, that the place would be crawling with security and police within minutes. In an environment where the presence of multi-million dollar actors, producers and directors was a daily occurrence, no one wanted strange men with guns running loose.

"We're going to back out the door now. If you follow, you can guess what happens to your friend."

The far man bowed his head in acquiescence. I released my grip on my prisoner's neck, prodding him once with the Draco. "Walk at my pace, stay between me and your friend." The man nodded in relief. "Sanit, you go first, careful to keep us between you and the gunman."

"Why don't we wait for the authorities?" she asked.

"Please, just do as I say." I had my reasons but was reluctant to share them.

We marched backward through the wide opening, swung left, and crabbed down the laneway another twenty yards until I was certain the first thug hadn't followed. Then, without warning, I raised the Draco and slammed the butt down hard on the side of my prisoner's head. The angle was awkward, but I knocked him to the ground, barely conscious.

"Nicholas, the other man will come after us now. What have you done?" asked Sanit.

"You're dead right," I responded. "Let's get the hell out of here."

Together, Sanit and I weaved our course out of the backlot and up through the theme park before finally reaching the parking area. It took a while. We had to stop regularly, changing direction, and sometimes doubling back to avoid roving patrols. The alarm raised, the whole site would now be on alert.

I knew Sanit questioned my decision, but to her credit, she didn't hesitate. When we reached the Jag, I threw the Draco onto the small back seat and pushed opened the passenger door for her. Before she climbed in, Sanit took a second to check over her shoulder.

"Nicholas, over there," she pointed to the western end of the car park. I turned my head. Through the rear screen, I saw our two Asian friends checking out each row of vehicles as they advanced towards us.

"Get in," I said.

Once in the car, Sanit pulled the door shut as I reversed out. Throwing the transmission into drive, I floored the gas pedal, releasing the power of the V-12. The screeching tires fought with the throaty roar of the engine as we headed up the lane of cars.

Sanit looked around again. "Nicholas, they've seen us." An edge of panic tremored in her voice.

As the Jag slid wildly around the end of our row onto the

57

main exit road, I responded.

"Perfect."

Chapter 11

The Jag's tires screeched again as I lurched left onto Coral Drive. As the car straightened up, I eased the pressure on the gas pedal.

"Nicholas, is there a problem?"

"All good," I replied.

Ten seconds later, a dark gray SUV pulled out from the car park in the same manner we had. Sanit turned around and gasped. She looked back at me, but to her credit said nothing. I picked up some speed, pushing the car close to its limit as we took the horseshoe bend at the top of Coral and onto Universal Studios Boulevard. The SUV dropped back. As we hit the Hollywood Freeway, I opened the Jag up, increasing our lead, but not by too much.

Once I was certain we'd set the pattern of the pursuit, I yanked my cell out of my jeans and pressed dial.

"Yup."

"You got them?"

"I've got them. Three hundred yards behind you heading north on the freeway, dark gray SUV."

I breathed a sigh of relief. "Excellent work, my friend."

"Hmph."

"And, Jack, keep your distance."

"As Connery once said, 'this ain't my first barbecue kid,'" came the response.

I hung up.

Sanit spoke up, "All right man of mystery, can you tell me what the heck is happening here?"

"Jack Greatrex has saved my butt more times than I can remember. Now he's saving yours," I replied.

I pushed harder on the gas pedal. We had to make a convincing show of trying to get away. I sneaked a quick look at Sanit. She didn't look the slightest bit mollified.

"All right," I began. "There was always a good chance things were going to go pear-shaped today. Your friends behind us are clearly not the sort who give up easily. It would have been great if the authorities could have settled things quickly at the park, but that didn't happen. If security or the police turned up undermanned, considering the firepower of those two thugs, someone was going to get hurt. We had to get out. Fortunately, I'd prearranged some extra help in case we needed it."

"Your friend is following the men following us?" she asked.

"Completely correct."

"But Nicholas, how is that going to help us escape?"

"In Iraq, we always played the long game, and we always had a plan."

"In Iraq?" I glanced over. Sanit's face had scrunched up in a look of confusion. I scoped out the road ahead before turning back toward her a few seconds later. The scrunch had gone, her demeanor more relaxed.

"So, Nicholas," she began, "just who the hell are you?"

We'd passed through Valley Glen and diverted left to join the Golden State Freeway, Interstate 5. The order of procession

60

and the distance between the vehicles hadn't changed.

I called Jack back, routing the call through the car speakers.

"Jack Greatrex, I'd like you to meet Sanit Mali."

"Pleased to meet you, Sanit," replied the big fella. "Sorry it's under such pressured circumstances."

Sanit seemed to hesitate. "Yes, you too, Jack. I don't quite know how to describe these circumstances, but they certainly are unusual."

As we passed through Mission Hills, the road rose. I tensed as I prepared for what had to come next.

"Are you ready, Jack?" I asked.

"On it," came a terse reply.

"Okay, here we go... game on."

The gas pedal hit the floor as the V12 surged forward. Jaguar XJS' were designed to chew roads like this, albeit in another era. We were doing close on one hundred miles an hour when we veered off at the Antelope Valley Highway. She held steady as a rock.

"Jack?"

"They've seen you and taken the turn, I'm on it now."

"Where are we going, Nicholas?" asked Sanit. Her voice revealing a slight quiver. I wondered if the speed worried her. It should, but what I planned next would worry her even more.

"It's not so much where we're going that's important, it's where they *think* we're going," I answered.

"But...?"

I decided that being mollified just wasn't Sanit's thing.

As we passed the Whitney Canyon Park on the left, I eased off the accelerator. The thugs following us may have had a newer car, but it was no V12. The gap between us was growing too big. I wanted to appear earnest, but not lose them.

"Catching up," Jack's voice came through the speakers loud and clear.

I eased the car to the right, losing a little more speed. The road was still good but becoming less smooth.

Suddenly we were running out of blacktop. Ahead of us, a T-intersection appeared. I eased slightly, before braking hard, losing speed rapidly. As I swung the wheel to the right, the rear of the car attempted to become the front. As soon as we'd rounded the apex of the corner, I floored the pedal. All twelve cylinders roared as they took control and the vehicle righted.

"Jack?"

"They've seen you turn. They're going around now. "Shit… didn't go as well for them. They've spun out, but they're not losing any time getting back on track."

As Greatrex spoke, the rear vision mirror reflected a metallic glint amongst a cloud of dust as the driver of the SUV wrestled his way off the dirt.

"Nicholas, this would have been easier at night. You've got to get the hell out of there."

"On it." The Placerita Canyon road wasn't constructed for the type of driving I had in mind. From the way Sanit clutched the armrest on the door with her left hand, and squeezed her seat with her right, neither was she. Too late to go back, we'd only have one chance at this. The Jag roared again.

Nicholas Sharp, channeling Lewis Hamilton… I hoped.

Every part of the vehicle seemed to strain as I took the next few corners. I glanced at the speedo: a little over eighty-five. Fifth bend in, the car's tail instigated a second attempt to take over the lead. I steered dissuasively into the skid.

"How does this end, Nicholas?" asked my terrified passenger.

"Well, I hope, but I really can't chat now."

A dirt embankment loomed before us, another hairpin bend demanding my attention. The rear wheels nudged the dirt but held steady.

"Jack, I'm about two miles off. You still there?"

"Yeah but hanging right back." Greatrex sounded more relaxed than I felt.

"I've lost them in my mirror, they must be somewhere between you and us," I said.

"Roger that."

"I'm just going to turn up the volume a bit, guarantee some distance."

A quick glance at Sanit told me all I needed to know. Her eyes were frozen wide in alarm; I imagine she thought me insane. Who could blame her? The car gave me more grunt as I rounded the next corner semi-sideways, the rear slewing out wildly. I was now driving to the full level of my ability, and a little beyond.

"Hang on, this bit could get hairy," I announced.

"Could?... why?... what are you going to do?"

There was no time to respond. I sensed the right wheels lift from the road as we tore around what was to be our final bend, not far out from the East Walker Ranch. I slammed my foot on the brake pedal three times in quick succession. The old Jag didn't have an advanced braking system, but it responded well to a racing stop. The speed fell off the vehicle, but she remained true. When we hit forty-five miles an hour, I heaved the wheel hard to the right.

The Jag jumped off the blacktop, leaving only sky visible through the windscreen. Sanit lost all inhibition and screamed.

I couldn't really blame her, a plunge down to the valley floor seemed inevitable. I held my breath as a split-second later the Jag's tires landed on a previously hidden gravel side road. The car fishtailed all over the dirt, violently objecting to the sudden change of surface and direction. It was a fight to control her, but slowly she settled. A half-mile along the path leading up into the foothills, we rolled to a stop. Fortunately, most of the dust we created remained shielded from the road by some dense scrub.

I glanced at Sanit. Her face was motionless apart from the slight tremor of her lower lip.

"Are you done?" she asked.

"I'm done."

"What now?"

"Just turn and watch."

As the words left my mouth, the dark gray SUV roared by at the bottom of the hill. It showed no sign of slowing.

"Your friend?"

"Watch."

A minute and a half later, Greatrex's white Nissan sauntered past. It stopped briefly when it reached the spot where we'd turned off. Jack Greatrex's bald head appeared out of the passenger window, his hand forming a 'thumbs up' position.

I wound down my window and returned the salute. As though a switch had been flicked, Greatrex's car revved loudly and took off down the canyon. The sound of its engine being thrashed to within an inch of its life resonated up the valley.

Sanit spoke first. "How did you know this track was here? There was no sign of it from the road."

"I used to hike the trails up here, with my dad," I replied.

She nodded her head, looking partially satisfied, before

stopping herself. "How long since you were last up here Nicholas?"

"Well, there's the thing," I responded. "I think the last time I walked these hills was about ten years ago."

If looks could kill.

Chapter 12

Neither of us spoke as we motored back along the Placerita Canyon road before heading back toward Santa Clarita. We'd turned north onto Interstate 5 before I broke the ice.

"See as how you're asking, there is a reason for this," I began.

Silence.

I continued. "It was important that we lost those two thugs. As long as they know where you are, you're in danger. Now, they have not only lost us, but I'm hopeful they'll assume we're heading in a completely different direction. I want them to focus somewhere else."

"Where do you believe they'll look?"

A response.

"It doesn't really matter where. They may figure we've headed back to San Bernardino and onto I-15 to get to Las Vegas, they may think we're heading to Death Valley, taking refuge in open spaces. To be honest, I don't really care."

"Where are we going?" Sanit asked.

"In a minute."

I pressed another contact on my cell. A woman answered, her voice warm and sultry. I felt a sharp intake of my own breath. "Nicholas."

"Kaitlin, it's going the way we thought it might," I responded.

A brief glimpse to my right showed a confused-looking expression on Sanit's face… again.

Kaitlin spoke again, "I've spoken to my step-father. It's fine for you to use the house. I'll call ahead to make the arrangements."

"Thanks Kaitlin, that's great," I replied.

"Nicholas," she continued, "he's very perplexed by what is happening here. He's looking into it."

"Tell him I'll call him when we get there," I responded. "And Kaitlin, there's one more thing I need to ask you. Please understand you are under no obligation to do this."

The phone was silent, although I was certain I heard the hint of a sigh at the other end.

"What do you need?" came the eventual response.

"Kaitlin, I can't stay up there with Sanit. Would you be able to meet us there?"

A few more seconds passed before she replied, "Of course."

"One more thing."

"What a surprise Nicholas, there always seems to be one more thing."

I flinched, and Sanit noticed, a tiny grin emerging from the side of her mouth.

"Kaitlin, I see no reason for there to be any danger up there, these people have no way of knowing where we're headed."

"But?"

"I want you to call Tommy Dabbs and take him up there with you."

"Why Tommy? We're well connected in law enforcement. There are any number of people we could call," Kaitlin replied.

"I understand that, but something is not making sense here. Until we can work this through, I want to stay off the grid. No-one official. Tommy can handle himself and he's resourceful. I know we haven't always seen eye to eye, but despite his colorful history, I trust him."

Another pause. "Yes, all right, I trust him too. I'll call him and we'll meet you up there."

The line went dead.

Sanit's bemused smile turned into a grin. "Girlfriend?"

"No… not really… I don't know. It's complicated." I responded.

"But you like her?" A smug silence followed Sanit's words as she waited for more information.

"Yeah, I like her, but there's a lot more to it," I offered.

She nodded her head. "All right. Now Nicholas, will you tell me where we're going?"

"There is a cabin, well out of the way, north of here. It's on Lake Almanor," I said.

Sanit looked at me quizzically, eyebrows tensing. "How far north?"

"A little over five hundred miles."

"Five hundred miles, that's hours away. We must find Dusit and Ram. We need to go back, now." There was a frustrated urgency in her voice.

"No Sanit. We need to get you somewhere safe, then I'll go back and search for the others."

The girl lent forward in her seat and raised her arms as though she was about to object, then she stopped. "I'm not some helpless little girl you know?"

"I'm aware of that Sanit, but knowing that you're safe frees us up to search for Dusit and Ram. It's a matter of available resources. Besides, we've already started," I answered.

"What do you mean?"

"As we speak, Jack Greatrex is following those thugs back to wherever they came from. Once he has a location, we may find out more about where Dusit and Ram are located and…" I paused for a second, uncertain how honest to be. "And what state they are in. I'm sorry to say it Sanit, but anything is possible."

She seemed to curl up into herself, just like she'd done in the studio. "I get it, but I'm just not ready to contemplate that possibility yet."

We drove on in a thoughtful silence before Sanit spoke again. "So who owns this house, the place hundreds of miles away. Is it your girlfriend-not girlfriend's stepfather? Who is he?"

"Kaitlin's, stepfather is former General Colin Devlin-Waters." I gripped the wheel tightly, bracing for the reaction to my next words. "He is the contact that put us in touch with the man at ICE."

As expected, Sanit exploded. "Are you stark raving mad? Do you have any idea what you've done? My friends are missing, maybe tortured, maybe dead, and you're taking me to the home of the man who betrayed them?"

The cocktail of grief, anger and anguish that flooded the car's cabin was so powerful I almost questioned my decision. Almost.

"Sanit, there are two men, and only two men on this planet who I would trust with my life, or yours. One of them is now risking his own wellbeing to tail a demonstrably violent pair of killer thugs who were trying to harm you and your friends. The other is General Colin Devlin-Waters, my former commanding officer in Iraq. He has saved my butt, and many others, countless times. I give you my word he did not betray you."

Sanit pushed herself back into her seat, lips pursed in anger. Twenty minutes of silence followed.

Eventually.

"Nicholas, as I said earlier today, I have no choice but to trust you, but it is not my way to give up control. In the past when I've done that, the cost has been high. I let Kamon decide how to protect us... me. And it cost him his life. Yet here I am giving in again. I pray you are right."

No sane man would interpret Sanit's response as being mollified, but I figured it was as close as I was going to get.

Ten minutes later, she spoke again. "Well, if we're going to be sitting together in this car for several hours, you'll have plenty of opportunity to unpack the story of Nicholas Sharp. Let's start with Iraq, then the general, your friend Jack, and perhaps the complicated world of the mysterious Kaitlin.

I pressed the gas pedal to the floor.

Chapter 13

"All right then, I'll go first."

My total inability to communicate with Sanit beyond mono-syllabic grunts for the initial hour of the drive had driven her to this point.

"I get it, Nicholas, I understand. You've put yourself, and your friends, at great risk to help our band... me, and I've given you little in return. Perhaps now is the time."

Flashes of light from oncoming headlights came and went as I concentrated on the road. Sanit was right, I didn't mind risking my own neck, but the game had changed, others were involved now.

"Go on." I offered a morsel of encouragement.

"I get the impression you have lived a difficult life Nicholas... complicated," she began. "I suspect we have that in common."

I snuck a glimpse at her across the dimly lit cabin. The next set of car lights revealed an expression of steely determination. Her words were not coming easily.

"To be honest, I'm not much of a sharer, not in the deeper sense. You may have noticed my habit of turning in on myself, kind of curling up."

"Mmm," I responded.

"It's a self-taught thing, a need to put the world on hold

while I figure out what's going on. I can tell you the date and time when the habit first started, but I really don't want to."

"You don't have to," I said. "Not for me."

"I believe I do. Well, maybe not the date and time, but perhaps the moment."

Sanit paused, nodding her head, finding the will to continue. I remained silent.

"They tell me that was the state they found me in, curled up in a corner of the garden of my family's home. I remember the night was wet, my dress was soaked through. I recall thinking I should come in from the rain, but I couldn't move until I'd made sense of what had happened."

"Sanit, you don't…"

"Shhh, if I stop, I won't restart."

Pause. I wondered if I'd blown it. I focused on the road, trying not to pressure her.

"In truth, I've never really made sense of the events of that night. Not even now. When they found me, they took me away. I remember people gasping when they moved me under the streetlight. At the time, their reaction surprised me.

My hands gripped tighter on the wheel.

"It turned out my dress was saturated in blood. I told them I wasn't ready to go, not until everything made sense."

"Were you badly hurt?" I asked.

"I was broken, completely broken. But I wasn't really hurt at all. The blood belonged to my father. I'd clung to him as he bled out. It was only a matter of seconds, but it was an awful lot of blood. They told me later that I couldn't have saved him, no matter what I did. I kind of already knew that.

"I'd watched the man enter our lounge room. He wore some regal kind of cloak and flowing robes. My father turned

72

around at his desk when he heard the footsteps. The man didn't even notice me playing Scrabble on the floor in a corner, behind a chair. I've always liked words. Without warning, before my father spoke, the man produced a small axe from under his robes."

Again, Sanit stopped talking. Another set of oncoming lights danced across the windscreen. Another glance in her direction. Just as she had on the trolley at Universal, she stared straight ahead... a private viewing of a past hell.

"I remember it so clearly. He held the axe in his right hand, up high. My father tried to back away, but he had nowhere to go. The man swung the axe from right to left, horizontal, across my father's neck, then back again the other way. Like some sort of ritual. My father collapsed onto the floor. There was so much blood Nicholas... so much.

When the man turned to leave, he saw me. He stared straight at me, through me. I remember being scared, angry and confused all at the same time. Does that seem odd to you?"

"Not in the slightest," I replied.

"Anyway, despite my fear, the man didn't kill me. He strolled toward me, his shadow towering over my Scrabble board. 'Let this be a lesson for you child. Don't be like your father; learn respect and silence.' Then he walked out. I thought it strange that he and my father had not uttered a single word to each other."

I nodded.

"Of course, I rushed straight over to my father and held him. Imagine that Nicholas, a ten-year-old girl witnessing the life drain away from her hero, her guiding star, the man she'd loved forever."

"Sanit, I'm so..."

"So I ran out to the garden and curled up in the rain… until things made sense. I guess I'm still curled up, still working things out. So that's where my music came from, anger, confusion, and perhaps a little fear. I discovered later my father was editor of a small underground newspaper, speaking truths against the government. That's why he was killed. His murderer had given me the best motivation ever, only he didn't mean to. As I grew older, I decided to never be scared into silence, and to respect only the truth. Then I found Kamon, Ram, and the others. Kha Cring was born and here we are."

I struggled to respond. This girl had the courage of a thousand warriors.

As we drove toward the darkness, I began to tell Sanit a little of my own story. It seemed to pale into insignificance now.

Chapter 14

Huge conifers stood like guardian angels, flanking the road as we wound along the Volcanic Legacy Scenic Byway between the Stove and Butte Mountains. The hours together had allowed Sanit and me a chance to understand each other. Somewhere between Stockton and Chico, I felt that we'd become friends.

We stopped at the small township of Chester to pick up some basic supplies before weaving our way around to the northern end of the lake towards the general's cabin. I knew from previous conversations with the 'great man' that his lakeside cabin was a refuge he didn't access enough. He lived in Maryland, just out of DC on the other side of the country, but he refused to give up his place on Lake Almanor.

As a precaution, I'd turned my cell off for most of the journey. Being out of touch with Greatrex while he worked the other end of the situation wasn't ideal, but we'd both agreed it was best to stay clear of any possible electronic tracking. I'd bought a throwaway cell phone in Chester when we purchased the supplies. Greatrex would do the same when he got a chance. We'd exchange numbers through Kaitlin. Better to be overcautious than dead.

The map app on the new phone had guided us effortlessly to

our destination. As we rounded the last bend, I realized that once again I'd underestimated the general. His 'cabin' turned out to be a sprawling home set on a picturesque hill beside the lake.

Sparsely populated in pines, the land on the right-hand side of the two-story weatherboard structure appeared to drop steeply to the lake. In the fading light, I made out a private pontoon reaching out into the glistening water. The general never did things by half.

Thicker forest surrounded the rest of the property. I caught glimpses of other houses through the trees, but the general's estate remained a secluded sanctuary. Although a long way from Los Angeles, the upmarket properties in the immediate area formed part of a gated enclave. Like all such places, respect for each other's privacy would be paramount. To prove the point, the armed security guard on duty as we'd passed onto the estate double-checked our identity and still made a call to Kaitlin to confirm we had permission to be there.

"Nicholas, this is beautiful," announced Sanit as she climbed out of the Jag. "In other circumstances…."

"Yes," I agreed, "this place is something special," but my mind focused elsewhere, scrutinizing the layout and approaches. Was this a defensible position? Not ideal, but doable. I had to stop myself and refocus on Sanit. The chances of us having to defend ourselves against any intruder were minimal. They simply had no idea of our location, and I intended to keep it that way.

Sanit pushed the door open to reveal a vast living space. The reclaimed wood-paneled walls framed an enormous stone fireplace that soared to the highest point of the cathedral ceiling. Opposite the fireplace, gigantic windows revealed a stunning view through the pines down onto the lake. A mezzanine level overlooked down over the expansive lounge.

Beside me, Sanit appeared stunned. "Oh, my…"

Before she finished her sentence, Sanit dashed up the wooden staircase to discover what else the house may reveal. Even if only briefly distracted, it was pleasing to see her smile. My own emotions slid in a different direction. I'd given Kaitlin my new cell number when I picked up the burner. She hadn't heard from Greatrex yet. The moment she and Tommy Dabbs arrived, I'd be back on my way to LA. At last contact, they remained about two hours away. I wasn't keen on the idea of another five-hour drive, but I enjoyed being out of contact with Greatrex less.

Sanit slept in an upstairs bedroom. I'd been sitting in the lounge alone for just over ninety minutes, caressing a small scotch into an evening's entertainment, when the front door burst open. I reacted instantaneously. On my feet and over the couch before the intruder's full body came into view, I had a chance, depending on what weaponry he or she carried… if there was only one of them. The man stepped forward. His wiry body belied the muscles I could see expanding the tattoos on his arms. His completely bald head and beard disguised his grim expression. The eyes pierced like death rays. Then his back up appeared.

My aggression muted; I froze.

"Hello Nicholas," said Tommy Dabbs. I suspected he'd secretly enjoyed the surprise entrance.

"I tried to stop him," said Kaitlin, smiling, "but he was having too much fun."

"You know that sort of behavior could get you hurt, Cupcake," I responded. Tommy wasn't too keen on his music industry nickname. It came out of his penchant for iced cupcakes, devoured at every opportunity. My initial response had been pathetic, but the startling entrance had irritated me. Sticks and stones.

Two seconds of silence drifted by, before we both burst out laughing.

"Good to see you, Nicholas."

"You too, Tommy, thanks for coming," I replied.

We shook hands and slapped each other on the back before I moved on to Kaitlin. As usual, her long blond hair framed her impenetrable brown eyes. Mystery and warmth in one sensuous package.

As I hugged her, I whispered, "thank you." She just nodded. Then I added, "Jack?"

Kaitlin released herself from my arms "Nothing, I'm sorry."

"You must be Kaitlin and Tommy." Sanit's voice crooned down from the mezzanine floor above us.

"And you would, of course, be Sanit," replied Kaitlin. I sensed a hint of ice in both their tones. Unexpected.

Sanit gracefully descended the staircase before shaking hands firmly with both Kaitlin and Tommy. We sat down on the couches surrounding the wooden coffee table. The sun long gone, the windows beside us now exposed nothing but darkness.

"I spoke to my stepfather on the journey up here. He's asked if you can call him," began Katlin.

"I was just about to," I responded. "Working this thing through in my own head has gotten me nowhere."

"I'm gonna take a walk," announced Tommy. "Get the lay of the land."

I nodded. "Good idea."

I got up, stepped over to the darkened window, found the switch, and lowered the blinds. I made a mental note to ensure Kaitlin and Sanit did the same for the rest of the house. No need to advertise our presence.

I pulled out my temporary cell and tapped in the General's number.

"It's Nicholas here, sir," I began.

"I'll get straight to the point, Nicholas. It is beyond my belief that Bill Stenton, my contact at ICE, would have alerted any strike team given the situation I described to him. It's equally unbelievable that he would have tipped off any agents or gangs as to your friend's whereabouts. I've known Bill for over thirty years, playing Judas is simply not in his DNA."

"I suspected as much," I replied. "The thing is, Sanit is certain they weren't followed. She, Dusit and Ram played an elaborate cat-and-mouse game between the studio and their apartment. Coming from the environment they have, the three of them have become quite adept at amateur, bordering on professional, fieldcraft. Besides that, they change apartments every week to guarantee their anonymity."

The general paused before replying. "You're on the ground there son, you have a better feel of what's going on than I do, but you know I can call in any number of people to help protect these kids if you say the word."

"I appreciate that general, but there are some issues at play here. First, we're uncertain if Dusit or Ram are even alive. Sanit hasn't heard from them by phone, and they failed to rendezvous at any of their prearranged meeting places."

"And?" asked the general, straight to the point.

"The second problem is that given the precautions these

kids have taken, and that you swear by your man, we simply don't know how these thugs keep tracking them down. Until we have that figured, I believe we need to hide Sanit away from the authorities and keep her off the grid." I didn't like my inference, but I had to make the point.

"I understand what you're saying Nicholas, but this really limits what we can do to protect Sanit, or locate her friends," replied my former commander.

"I know sir, and that's what worries me."

"Have you or Kaitlin had any contact from Jack?" he asked.

"Not a word, so that brings another complication. Under normal conditions, Jack would be too smart to be spotted tailing a target, but he's operating alone, not as part of a surveillance team. That increases his exposure tenfold." My guilt about Greatrex's involvement increased as I spoke.

"You're going back to LA, aren't you?" asked the General.

"Yes sir, I am."

"On your own?"

"Yes, sir."

"I'll do what I can from this end, although my usefulness is limited by the scenario you've just inferred. For God's sake Nicholas, be careful."

"Yes, sir." I hung up.

I jumped when Kaitlin put her hand on my shoulder. I looked up to see her comforting smile. "It *will* be all right. Jack knows what he's doing, and you guys seem to sense what the other is thinking even when you can't speak."

I hoped to hell she was right.

Kaitlin paused. "Sanit certainly is a beautiful young woman." Ahh.

The door banged behind me and Tommy Dabbs strolled

80

back into the room. Tommy never seemed to walk or run anywhere, always a leisurely meander.

"I've checked the entire block out, there are better places to hold up, but there could be worse."

Tommy spoke with a reassuring confidence.

"There is almost no chance they'll find out about this place, Tommy. I'm just being overly cautious."

"From the little I know about your past Nicholas, I'd say that's probably how you've stayed alive this long," he replied.

As I nodded a response, Sanit walked over.

"What now, Nicholas?" she asked.

Worried to the core about her friends, she had the good grace not to push me. If she'd known me better, she'd have known she didn't have to.

"I'm going back to LA, tonight," I announced.

"Nicholas, you're dog tired, and it's not an easy road at the best of times," said Kaitlin.

"I'm going," I repeated. I reached down, grabbed my bag, and marched forward to the door. Kaitlin and Tommy knew better than to attempt to dissuade me, and Sanit didn't want to.

"I've got this," said Tommy. "Don't you worry about a thing up here, we're good."

I nodded again.

Kaitlin and Sanit stood motionless.

"Don't say a word," I said to them all, before turning and walking into the night.

Chapter 15

For me, driving is therapy. Late at night, a long winding road, the Jag, a perfect panacea. Staying on the asphalt took all my attention as I pushed my way down toward the interstate. I'd turned south at Chico, onto the Golden State Highway, before I allowed my thoughts to wander.

I had every confidence in Greatrex's ability to stay on top of the situation, but I still hadn't heard from him. That continued to worry me. The burner phone on the seat next to me remained silent, and I wouldn't turn my own cell back on until I was well clear of the area.

Nicholas Sharp, man of caution. Many would disagree.

I shoved my uneasiness about the big fella to one side and concentrated on other concerns. First Dusit and Ram. Were they alive? If they had been killed, wouldn't the authorities have found their bodies? Not necessarily. LA concealed plenty of places where a couple of bodies could remain undiscovered. I wondered if the two musicians were being held captive somewhere. These kids appeared streetwise; they'd been through too much not to be. If they'd been able to, their first reaction would have been to contact Sanit. Now under-wraps hundreds of miles away, Sanit would prove difficult to reach. That had seemed like a good idea at the time, but was it?

I powered down the highway, joining Interstate 5 at Sacramento. I drove quickly, my heavy right foot a developing habit.

Thoughts leaped around my head like subatomic particles orbiting their nucleus. In this case, the nucleus was the truth. What lay behind all of this? Why did a foreign country risk so much by sending agents to kidnap or kill a group of protest musicians? But *were* they really risking that much? If they worked with a US state-sponsored group or government agency, then the foreign agents really risked nothing. But how the hell did such a relationship develop?

The busy highway traffic acting as a constant distraction, I weaved my way toward LA. I focused intensely on the road ahead, almost hoping the blacktop itself would present an answer.

Then it did. The light bulb flicked on, albeit dimly. I picked up my burner and dialed 4-1-1, directory assistance.

"The number for the Culver City Police Department, please. No, it's not an emergency, yes please connect me."

A minute later, a phone rang somewhere in Culver City.

"Culver City Police, how can I direct your call?"

"Can you put me through to the Investigation Bureau, please?"

"Yes sir, just a moment."

More ringing before a weary voice answered.

"Investigation."

"Detective Michael Alroy, please."

"Hang on." The tired, I presumed detective, on the end of the line, barely made any attempt to cover the mouthpiece. "Is Alroy still around?"

I waited, making the most of the traffic's distraction. The

voice came back on.

"Alroy's left, sorry. Can I take a message?" He sounded like he didn't want to.

"Can you tell him Nicholas Sharp called? I gave him the burner cell's number. It's quite urgent."

"Sure." The line went dead.

Life is full of surprises, and I received one three minutes later when the burner vibrated next to me.

"Sharp."

"Sharp, it's Alroy, I just got your message. What's up?"

"Thanks for the swift response, Detective."

"Yeah, Higgins sounds a little slack over the phone, but he knew I'd been working on your case. He passed the message on pretty-damn quick. Has something turned up?"

"No, not really," I replied, "but I've got a question for you."

"Shoot."

"After you questioned us at the studio, did any other department or authority call you to express any interest in the case?"

Alroy paused, trained to think before answering. "No, nothing unusual that I recall. Until the attack on the band's apartment, this appeared to be a pretty straightforward situation from our end. Of course, things have certainly ramped up now."

I felt myself deflate, sighing in defeat. I froze half-way through the sigh. "When you say ramped up, what exactly do you mean?" I asked.

"Well, suddenly everyone wants in on this. They're all saying there are national security implications and possible international ramifications. Everyone bar the Los Angeles Sanitation Bureau seems to want to either be involved or reported to. There's more traffic here than on the interstate, and to be honest, it's giving me the shits."

I appreciated Alroy's candor, but the information didn't help. For my theory to make sense, someone else needed to be active on the case *before* the shooting at the apartment block. I'd gotten myself needlessly excited, grasping at straws.

"Thanks Detective, I appreciate the call, but I think I'm on the wrong track," I responded.

"No worries Sharp, I assume you are looking after Ms. Mali, Mr. Salae and Mr. Chanthora. I would expect you've received several calls from all sorts of department heads trying to chase them down. I planned on calling you myself tomorrow, once the traffic clears, so to speak."

My turn to pause, choose my words wisely. My gut told me I could trust Alroy, but the same conflicted gut said trust no-one. "Detective, I understand Sanit is safe, but she is not with me." Technically not a lie. "I don't know where Dusit and Ram are, and it worries me you don't either."

"Good point, but Sharp, be careful. People are throwing money and attention at this."

"Thanks Detective, I'm sure we'll be talking," I replied, before hanging up.

I drove on, my thoughts divided between the cars ahead and Alroy's words. A lot of agencies had their heads in the picture now. Perhaps I was batting out of my league. Should I have taken Sanit straight to the authorities, but if so, which authority?

As I continued to wrestle with too many pestering questions, my glimmering light bulb moment turned into a lightning strike. I hadn't understood why the thugs coming after Sanit, Dusit and Ram made such a big thing of shooting up their apartment block. The young musicians could have been kidnapped or worse, a lot more quietly. But now, I realized that was the whole point. They needed to create a major situation that would justify all these agencies becoming involved. My certainty grew by the minute. There had to be one agency with their face in the trough that placed their own agenda above the wellbeing of the members of Kha Cring. The question remained, which agency, and what in God's name was *their* agenda?

Dangerously out of hand and increasingly complicated, I now found myself stuck slap in the middle of a huge shitstorm. If that weren't bad enough, I'd positioned Greatrex directly beside me.

Right foot down and seven hundred and fifty horses roared into the night.

Chapter 16

When I hit the Bakersfield area, I turned my own phone back on. My location would give nothing vital away now. Twenty-seven messages awaited my attention. So, suddenly I'm popular. I worked my way through them, Detective Alroy had been right. It seemed like every human in LA with some involvement in law enforcement wanted to get hold of me. ICE, Homeland Security, LAPD, the FBI, and more. Uncertain who to call, I called no one. Two messages from Alroy. No need to return those either.

The second last message hit the ticket. Jack Greatrex: "Nicholas, call me." I nearly wept with relief as my guilt jumped ship. I pressed dial.

"Nicholas."

"Jack, what the hell? Where have you been? I've been worried sick," I replied.

"Yeah, sorry about that, although I suppose I appreciate the angry mum thing."

"So where are you?" I asked.

"On my way home to do some research."

"I'm coming into LA now," I said. "I'll meet you at my place. Did you tag those two thugs?"

"Yeah, I'll tell you more when I see you." Greatrex never

really enjoyed talking on the phone.

An hour later, I hauled into the parking lot under my block. As I climbed the stairs, Greatrex stood waiting outside my apartment.

"You're not going to like it," he announced.

"Like what?"

The big fella stepped aside and swept his arm toward my door, or to be more accurate, the remains of my door.

"Shit."

"I told you."

Attached to the frame by a single hinge, the front door sagged sadly to one side. I walked past Greatrex into my lounge. The room had been done over. They had ripped every draw out. The books that had been neatly arranged in my bookcase now lay strewn across the floor. The kitchen area looked like a grenade had exploded. The only saving grace being my black Yamaha grand piano appeared intact, bar its stool smashed to pieces.

I marched into my bedroom, then the spare, only to find a similar scenario. By the time I returned to the lounge, Greatrex had put the cushions back on the couch and had replaced some books into the bookshelves.

"I didn't see any point waiting for the cops to fingerprint the place," he said.

I slumped down onto the couch. "No, none at all. This is the work of a professional. Besides, which cops would I call?"

Greatrex raised an eyebrow but didn't request an explanation.

He poured us both a scotch and passed me a glass before sitting in the chair opposite.

"This is getting beyond nasty," he said.

"It got way beyond nasty when Sonny was murdered in that alley behind the studio," I responded.

"Is Sanit okay?" he asked.

"As of when I left Lake Almanor, she was fine," I replied. "We can call them in a minute, but first, what happened with you and the two guys you were chasing?"

"Well, there's a bit of a story there. I reckon I've driven half-way across California in the last twelve hours or so. Initially, they did what you expected and hit the road to Vegas. About a third of the way there, they changed their minds and backtracked to the Placerita Canyon road where they'd lost you. They poked around there for a while, before heading north. That worried me, but suddenly for no apparent reason, they came back into LA."

"They didn't see you and flipped directions to ditch the surveillance?" I asked.

"No, they seemed too purposeful and direct in their driving. No litany of unnecessary turns to shake a tail. At that point, I figure they had no idea," the big fella replied.

"At that point?"

"I'll come to that," he continued. "I followed them back to Echo Park. I ran into trouble when they pulled into a gated estate."

Clearly, I wasn't the only one who thought a gated estate provided some level of protection.

"What did you do?" I asked.

"For a moment, I suspected they may have caught me in their mirror. They'd stopped at the guardhouse at the estate entrance. When I rounded the last corner, I had to make out like I intended pulling into a driveway. Trouble being, the owner appeared, so I had to reverse and double back the way I came in. It might have been a giveaway."

"Don't beat yourself up, a one-man surveillance over those distances is as much luck as procedure," I replied.

"Either way, that's when things got interesting. I parked the car and jumped a couple of fences. With the estate being gated and all, I figured I had a pretty good chance of finding out where they went. Standard routine with those places, only one entry point."

"Go on."

"Well, a few minutes later I spotted their vehicle in a driveway. A huge two-story place. High walls, floodlit gardens and security cameras on the fence and at every corner of the building within sight."

"Please tell me you didn't go in." I pleaded.

"I needed a quick look, to check if your new friends Dusit and Ram were held inside," Greatrex said.

"Jack?"

"Don't say you wouldn't have done the same, Nicholas."

I shrugged my shoulders. Jack Greatrex and I knew each other too well.

"I didn't hear from you for hours, so I'm assuming something happened?" I asked.

"Well, yeah. I'd taken my own cell with me and left the burner in the car. My phone had a better camera."

"And..."

"I made it around the back of the garage undetected. The garage itself was huge, at least six cars. It turned out the drapes at the rear of the house had been opened. The bad news is that while I sat there snapping away through the rear windows, they sent out six guys, all similar build to our thug friends, to guard the perimeter. They blocked my exit. I remained stuck, hunched in a bush behind that damn building for four hours."

I chuckled. The image of Greatrex stuck in a bush was comic, the frustration he would have felt, palpable. I must have chuckled too loudly.

"Thanks for your support," came the big fella's terse reply, but he smiled. "Of course, I didn't intend calling you or Kaitlin using my own phone. Better to keep you off the radar."

"Sorry. So, did you see Dusit and Ram?"

"From how you described them, I'm thinking no. Several men of Asian heritage wandered around, but they appeared either the wrong age or to be obvious bodyguard types."

Disappointment stirred within. It would be nothing compared to how Sanit would react.

Greatrex continued. "After a couple of hours, things suddenly went from boring to weird. All the outside lights flicked off. Two cars pulled up out front. From where I perched, I couldn't see them, but I heard the engines revving and the guards talking to someone, followed by some radio chatter. A few minutes later, four guys in dark suits walked into the rear lounge room. They looked to be Caucasian and held themselves like professionals. I raised the phone to get some pictures, but someone must have pressed a button somewhere and the drapes automatically closed. I got off a couple of fleeting shots, but they're of little use."

Greatrex pulled out his cell. He showed me several photographs. They were poorly lit images of four men in dark suits. The only faces I could make out clearly were the Asian thugs who, presumably, had already been in the house. I flicked briefly through the big fella's other photos, which confirmed it.

"Nicholas, you may think this odd, but in the brief time I had those guys in view, I had a feeling about them. When I say they were suits, I really mean suits. They carried themselves in that same matter of fact, 'no one can touch me' manner that..."

"Feds and cops do," I finished my friend's sentence.

"Exactly, but it's just a hunch."

Too many times in my life I'd been saved by Jack Greatrex's feelings and hunches. I learned to trust them like truth itself.

"I waited another twenty minutes. When it became obvious nothing more was going to happen, I used the darkness to hasten my retreat. I made it back to the car, got out of there fast, and called you."

For ten minutes, Greatrex and I sat in my lounge processing the mine of information. My own hunches regarding the involvement of some sort of outside influence seemed to firm up. A worrying turn of events. But Federal agents, cops? Where the hell was this going?

"Of course, Feds could mean FBI, Homeland Security, ICE, or a zillion others. We simply don't know," I said.

Every conversation I'd had since walking into that recording studio a couple of days earlier replayed in my head. Sanit, Dusit, Ram, Alroy, Sergeant Stone at the apartments. All their words spun around like some kind of cipher. I just couldn't find the damn key.

More minutes slipped by, my thoughts swirling around the eye of a storm. We both wanted to act, but how? Abruptly the clouds parted.

"Oh my God... no." I leaped to my feet. "Jack, we're leaving now. I just hope we're not too late."

Greatrex jumped up and followed me out through the

damaged doorway without question. I expected no less, but I owed him an explanation.

"'More traffic here than on an interstate'," I yelled.

I glanced over my shoulder to see Greatrex's face, a twisted mass of confusion.

"What?" he said.

"Alroy told me that more people and agencies had become involved in this than he would have expected. His actual words were: 'more traffic here than on the interstate'."

"So?"

"Jack, when I spoke to Alroy I was driving down Interstate Five, but he already knew that. My car is being tracked. If they know where I am, they know where Sanit, Kaitlin and Tommy are. I may as well have invited the bad guys along."

As Greatrex's Nissan thundered out of the car park, with me at the wheel, I pulled my cell from my pocket and dialed Kaitlin's number. Then I tried Tommy's. Then I tried Sanit. No answer from any of them. I chucked the phone onto Jack's lap.

"Keep trying. Also try the local police, anybody close enough."

Greatrex worked the phone frantically.

I hoped to God, any God, that we would make it there in time. The alternative was unfathomable.

Chapter 17

TOMMY DABBS

Tommy Dabbs stared into the blackness. Listening. A sharp snap cut through the silence. A twig underfoot? Then nothing. Tommy couldn't be sure of anything in this environment. Raised in East LA, the jungle he grew up in existed a world away from the forest that surrounded this luxury retreat. His jungle comprised concrete, gangs, and too much violence. Tommy peered into the gloom. He'd scanned the layout of the property, the lake at the foot of the slope, the long driveway, the surrounding thick scrub, but with no moon tonight, he had little but his ears to hint at any untoward presence.

Of course, Tommy's ears had become his pot of gold, they'd helped him drag himself out of the world of gang culture. Certain how his life would end if he stayed, he figured his mother's heart would break when the police eventually came to her door, explaining Tommy's last hours on this earth. He wouldn't let that happen to her. He loved his mom.

Another crack echoed through the garden. Now sure he'd identified a breaking twig, Tommy still wasn't overly alarmed. Chances were the sound came from a wild beast of some sort. He didn't understand the local animals here like he did the human ones in the streets of LA. In the city, he understood their motivation, their instinct for survival. Perhaps things weren't so different up here after all.

Tommy moved along the veranda toward the eastern corner. Still unable to see anything, he played with the idea that a couple of shadows had shifted position in the darkness. He concentrated his gaze. They weren't moving now. He needed to stow his imagination and rely on his ears. Yes, he trusted his ears. His music teacher at school, for the few days a week he attended, told him he had naturally good ears, perhaps even perfect pitch. Tommy's family couldn't afford the expensive instrumental tuition that his teacher suggested, so she organized free lessons. He chose the bass guitar; he liked the sound and feel of the instrument. But in the end, he'd spent so few days at school, they dropped him from the program. Anyway, he belonged to the streets, not some 'up themselves' institution.

Tommy's older brother was killed in a turf war between their gang and a group from the western side of town. The grief galvanized Tommy into realizing his life needed to change. Aware his school days had passed him by, he found a job doing the only thing he was qualified to do. Lift things.

He started work with a freight company, somehow that led to him helping a few local bands load their gear into venues. He hung around their shows and became interested in how all the equipment functioned. A local sound guy noted his interest and gave him a chance. One night, he asked Tommy to operate the band's fold-back system. Fold-back is how the musicians hear themselves when they perform. After the first show, the band told the sound guy that Tommy created the best onstage sound they'd ever worked with. A career born.

His ears carried him forward. Who would have thought?

After fifteen motionless minutes with no further sounds, Tommy decided to retreat inside to Kaitlin and the girl, Sanit. He had all the time in the world for Kaitlin. She'd saved him when things went wrong and he'd stupidly regressed after doing some minor drug dealing on the side. He hadn't meant for that to happen, but of course the cops didn't believe a word he said. Kaitlin saved his ass. After a short stint locked up, nobody wanted to hire Tommy, his brief career torpedoed before it began. Ears or not, Tommy's only choices lay back on the streets. Out of the blue, Kaitlin, who'd become a high-level tour manager by then, offered him one short tour, an opportunity to prove his worth. The gig worked out. Tommy would do anything for her, that's why he was here.

Tommy knew Kaitlin liked Nicholas Sharp. Tommy didn't mind Sharp either. He was a bit of a smartass, but a crazy wild musician. Besides, Tommy liked the fact Sharp had a past that people only spoke about in hushed tones. That was cool.

Stopping by the front door, Tommy listened carefully one more time. He stood motionless, straining for any hint of something being wrong. Another sharp crack resonated up the hill. It would have to have been a hell of a large wild animal to break a twig like that. His ears hadn't let him down after all.

Tommy slipped silently back into the house. Kaitlin and Sanit sat on the couch talking. "Problem ladies, someone's out there. It could be nothing, but someone is definitely out there," he announced. Tommy never pulled his punches, verbal or otherwise.

Kaitlin Reed reacted first. "Tommy, if people are outside and they haven't knocked on the door yet, it can't be good."

Of course, Kaitlin was right. Tommy looked at Sanit. She shook nervously around, before kind of willing herself to calm down. Strong.

"All right, how do we get out of here?" she asked.

Tommy didn't have an answer, but he wouldn't let anything happen to these two. He reached down into a canvas bag he'd left next to the door. He plucked out a pair of small pistols, passing one to each of the girls.

"Either of you know how to shoot?"

"I do," replied Kaitlin, "my stepfather taught me."

Of course she did, thought Tommy.

Kaitlin continued, "I'll show Sanit the basics."

Tommy reached back into his bag. He pulled out a semi-automatic Remington 700. The weapon had aged, but its aim remained true. Both girls look surprised.

"It's okay, ladies. The gun's registered to me." He figured they didn't believe him, but right now they didn't care. Tommy always had trouble living completely within the law. "Both of you get down behind the couches. Sanit, you aim at the big window, Kaitlin you aim at the door. If anyone comes through either entrance, don't hesitate, just shoot."

"What if it's you, Tommy?" asked Kaitlin.

"It won't be," he replied. Suddenly Tommy sensed he wouldn't be stepping back into this house... ever. Shoving the sensation out of his mind, he flicked off the lights and slid quietly out the doorway. He would do anything for Kaitlin.

Crouched low behind the balcony railing, Tommy was aware the narrow wooden beams offered no protection, but the shape might disguise his movements. He could have swung off the other end of the deck and tried to edge a path behind whoever lurked in the shadows, but that would leave the door and the girls exposed. Not going to happen. For a fleeting moment, it occurred to Tommy that Sharp might be pleased with his strategy. He inched further along the railing until he found a position squatting down at the corner of the veranda. Even if the blinding darkness prevented him from seeing anything, he could listen clearly from both directions. He'd been in some gunfights before, with his older brother, but not like this. Either way, look how that turned out.

For fifteen minutes Tommy didn't move. He barely breathed. Was that another snap coming from down the hill toward the water? He wasn't certain. Another five minutes passed before he caught the first moving shadow. A figure crept down the edge of the driveway. Tommy watched the figure crouch behind his own bright red pickup. Of course, in the dim light, the vehicle didn't look bright red now.

If it was just one man, this might work out all right. Tommy was a sure hand with the Remington. As the thought passed, another figure appeared down the northern side of the drive. Damn. The shadow moved from bush to bush, deadly silent and barely noticeable. A glimmer of light split through the clouds, the outline of some sort of rifle in the figure's hands alarmingly clear.

To his left, Tommy recognized the gentle crunch of dried pine needles. Once more, he peered down into the blackness towards the lake. A hint of moonlight now reflected off the water's surface. He noticed a figure slip silently from one tree to take refuge behind another. He glimpsed the figure again, only this time it cowered behind a different tree. How did the figure move so quickly? Suddenly Tommy realized the original figure hadn't shifted position at all. There were two people on the slope.

Shit. That meant a total of at least four of them approaching the house.

Certain he remained unseen, Tommy figured he held the element of surprise. But he didn't have a plan to deal with all four of them. Besides, who knew what the hell was happening on the other side of the house? He wished Sharp was here, with his mate Greatrex. That would even up the odds, but they were miles away in LA. What was Sharp thinking?

The next sound jolted Tommy like an electric shock. Almost silently, but not quite, a leather sole scratched on the first wooden plank of the veranda steps. Now or never.

Tommy swung the Remington around and squeezed the trigger. As he fired, the flash of light from the muzzle revealed a large man doubling forward. Gutshot. Two more quick bursts and the figure rose in the air before plummeting backward down the steps to the ground. Good. One down…

As Tommy turned the gun toward the shadow on the left-hand side of the drive, hell itself descended upon him. What used to be the balcony rail morphed into a hail of splintered wood flying in all directions. A sharp stabbing sensation flooded through his left arm.

So that's what being shot felt like.

Just as well they hit his left arm. Tommy kept swinging the rifle around, spraying the garden and the forest with a shower of lead. Another figure collapsed on the ground. Little point in saving ammunition now.

As he fired, Tommy rose to his feet, going for a better angle of fire. More shadows reacted, silently closing in on the house. Tommy held his finger on the trigger, firing a random spray across the grounds. Damn, the Remington was a good weapon, you could count on it.

Suddenly, like thunder, the clapboards behind him disintegrated under a massive onslaught of firepower, showering him with splinters. Things seemed to be going to shit, but Tommy didn't panic, he never panicked. He'd gotten off two more quick bursts before the hail of bullets ripped into his torso, smashing him hard against the wall of the house. Momentarily surprised at the sensation of numbness rather than pain, Tommy attempted to keep firing. His gun lay next to him, flat across the veranda's floorboards, his finger still wrapped around the trigger. He tried squeezing his hand tight. He should re-aim, but it took every morsel of energy to raise the weapon a single inch. Why weren't his limbs responding?

Tommy sensed the moistness soak through him. He had a perception of drowning in a glistening dam flowing with his own blood. Still, he protected the front door. If he could only get off another round, it might be okay.

Out of the darkness, an enormous shadow loomed before him. Tommy understood what that meant. But what about Kaitlin, what about the girl? He'd do anything for Kaitlin.

Where the hell is Sharp?

Tommy Dabbs, the man with golden ears, didn't even hear the final volley of gunfire that ended his life.

Chapter 18

"When you get to Sherman Oaks, turn right onto the Ventura Freeway," Greatrex commanded.

"But that's not the quickest route," I responded.

"It's the quickest route to the airport."

I'd been concentrating on the road rather than Greatrex's calls, but now the penny dropped.

"Eddie Small?" I asked.

"He'll be waiting, ready to go."

An old buddy of Greatrex's, Eddie Small, ran a helicopter charter business out of Hollywood Burbank Airport. He'd helped us out before.

"It's got to be faster than driving," I said, "but will it be fast enough?"

As we pulled into the airport parking lot, my phone chirped. Greatrex passed it over. Kaitlin's number appeared on the screen. He'd been trying it constantly between his other calls.

I screamed into the phone, "Kaitlin, they know where you are. Get out of there now!"

"Nicholas, I think they're here. There's someone outside, Tommy's gone out to check." The chill that ran through me would have made the arctic seem tropical.

"Okay, make sure you lock everything and the drapes are

closed. Jack's been onto the local law enforcement in Chester, they're on their way to you as we speak."

I heard Kaitlin's sigh of relief through the phone. "How long until they arrive?"

"They said about twenty minutes, ten minutes ago," I replied.

"Nicholas," Kaitlin sounded on edge again, "it may be too late by then."

"Kaitlin, the Chester cops may be a small police force, but they're professionals, they'll look after you," I reassured her. I kicked myself for not alerting the locals earlier. It had seemed unnecessary.

"I've got to go, Sanit…"

I had to pull my phone away from my ear as a staccato of gunfire pounded out of the speakers.

"Kaitlin… Kaitlin what's happening?"

The line went dead.

Without doubt, the next hour of the journey became one of the miserable intervals of my life. We'd heard nothing more from anyone at the cabin. We couldn't even get any clarity from the Chester Police Department. 'There had been a situation at a residence at Lake Almanor and officers were attending' remained the official comment.

Fifty-seven minutes after my conversation with Kaitlin had ended so abruptly, my phone chirped again.

"Kaitlin, are you all right?" I was uncertain that it was even Kaitlin on the other end of the call. It could have been a cop, about to break bad news.

"Yes Nicholas, I'm sort of okay." Relief. Her tone, however, told a different story. She sounded remote, distant. "Nicholas, Tommy is dead," she said matter-of-factly.

"Shit… Sanit?"

"Gone, they took her."

"Are you hurt?" I asked.

"Not enough to be concerned," came the terse reply.

"Are the cops in control of the scene now?"

"Yes." One-word answers.

I felt partially relieved to have the sit-rep, at least Kaitlin was in safe hands. The rest of the news kicked like a mule. Tommy Dabbs dead. I'd done that, my fault. Sanit taken, my fault. Kaitlin put in harm's way. I'd asked her to come.

"Kaitlin, we're still a couple of hours out. Please, just do what the police ask. We'll see you soon," I said.

"Okay." Silence. The call ended.

As we flew on into the sunrise, there was nothing more Greatrex and I could do… yet. The big fella had some questions, so I tried to give him some answers.

"Tell me exactly how you figured they had a tracker on you."

"As I mentioned, Detective Alroy's statement gave it away. When he said, 'more traffic here than on an interstate', I'd just assumed he'd referred to the number of agencies involved in the investigation."

"Go on."

"I didn't get it until you started talking about the 'suits' at the place in Echo Park. If outside agencies swamped the case, their own suits would have been everywhere, including with Alroy. If they played this as a big-time event, no one would head home to sleep," I said.

"So, you reckon Alroy would have had some feds with him, but didn't want to say," suggested Greatrex.

"Exactly, and the only reason he didn't want to mention anything would have been because he didn't trust them." I continued. "That's why he dropped the 'interstate' reference, to let me know I was being monitored.

"He wanted you to turn around and get the hell back up to Almanor."

"You've got it," I responded. "But I didn't get it soon enough."

A hint of the upcoming sunrise peeped over the horizon as the chopper touched down on the golf course near the General's cabin. We said our goodbyes to Eddie and alighted onto the grassy space.

Two uniformed officers from the Chester Police presented themselves.

"Mr. Sharp and Mr. Greatrex?"

We nodded.

"Come with us, please. Our Lieutenant is extremely keen to speak with you both."

No surprises there. We followed the police officers to their car. Three minutes later, we pulled up at the driveway leading to the general's cabin.

The sunrise had risen just enough for us to absorb the scene. What had been a tranquil rustic escape the evening before, now looked like a warzone. The balustrade that circled two sides of the house had been smashed into a mess of mangled firewood. Hundreds of bullet holes pocked the brick parts of the wall, the timber sections obliterated.

Police tape marked off the driveway and most of the distance along the front of the property. One of our guardian officers raised the tape to let us through. As we walked up the driveway, I noted a sheet covering what I assumed to be a body. It lay to one side of the red pickup that sat in the drive. Tommy Dabbs' pickup. As we strode closer to the building, I noticed another body perched on a bed of pine needles in the conifer forest to the lake side of the house.

I glanced at Greatrex. His creased brow and pursed lips showed a similar reaction to mine. We'd seen all of this before, but in the remote villages of Iraq, not an upmarket resort in California.

Laying a couple of yards back from the front steps was a third corpse, again covered with a sheet. If Tommy Dabbs alone had inflicted all this damage, he'd done one hell of a job.

Tommy Dabbs. The fourth body lay slumped across the cabin's front doorway, its shoulders resting on the shattered door jamb. We didn't need to be told. Despite the sheet covering the figure, I knew this would be Tommy. The sight of his last stand. No soldier worth their salt takes pleasure in death, but when you've lost one of your own, it's a different kick in the guts. Tommy was one of our own.

The officer to my left tapped my shoulder, breaking me from my dark thoughts. "The lieutenant requested that we enter through the back door. Ms. Reed is inside. Apparently, she's refused to leave the scene until you arrive, Mr. Sharp."

I nodded. Greatrex and I followed him around to the rear of the building.

"Mr. Sharp, Mr. Greatrex, I'm Lieutenant Alan Shepard of the Chester Police Department." A tall slender man, wearing a gray suit and a somber smile greeted us at the back door. "Before you come in, I must ask you not to touch anything. This is, of course, a crime scene that we're still processing. I have several questions of you both, but I'm sure you would rather see Ms. Reed first."

"Yes, please lieutenant," I responded.

The police officer continued, "I should warn you that Ms.

Reed seems extremely shaken up by this. She will need time to come to terms with last night's events."

"Thank you, lieutenant." Shepard led us down the hallway. His description of Kaitlin's reaction was perplexing. Obviously, these events would shake anyone to their core, but Kaitlin had seen too many perilous situations for her to crumble so easily. On the other hand, the human spirit can only handle so much.

The lieutenant turned off the hallway into a large master bedroom. Kaitlin sat in an armchair in a small sitting area by the window. When she looked up, I noted a flash of relief pass across her face before her shoulders slumped back into the chair.

"Nicholas, Jack."

I walked over, squatted on the edge of her chair and wrapped my arm around her shoulders. She leaned her head toward me. Jack crouched down in front of the chair.

"Lieutenant, would you mind giving us a few minutes?" I asked the officer at the door.

He nodded. "Sure thing," he said, before turning away.

I moved off the arm and stood, taking Kaitlin's left hand in mine as I gazed down at her. Her hair fell chaotically across her face, disheveled. The streaks of what little makeup she wore told me there had been tears. It took me a moment to realize that 'had been' was the operative term. Kaitlin glanced at the door, ensuring the lieutenant had left, before her eyes brightened and her jaw edged forward in a sign of dogged determination.

"Nicholas, we need to talk."

Chapter 19

"Don't get me wrong," she began. "I'm beyond gutted that Tommy is dead. He was a good man, and he did everything within his power to protect Sanit and me."

"I'm sorry I dragged you and Tommy into this," I replied. "I thought it would be a simple babysitting job. If I had any idea, they'd be able to track us to this location, I would never have involved you."

Kaitlin looked up at me with a stare that pierced my soul. "I'm sure you wouldn't Nicholas. This turned out to be bigger than any of us figured, Tommy included." She squeezed my hand.

Greatrex then said what I wanted to say. "Kaitlin, of course we're all upset about Tommy's death, and worried as all hell about Sanit and her friends, but..."

"But why the frail girl at the end of her tether act?" she asked.

I responded. "Exactly."

"I'll go through everything that has gone down here in a minute, but first I need to tell you, I'm concerned about the people in the next room."

"Why so?" inquired the big fella.

"There can be no way the Chester Police Department had any untoward involvement in all of this," I added.

Kaitlin leaned forward and whispered. "Yes, I agree, but it's not the local police I'm concerned about."

Greatrex and I waited for her to elaborate.

"Nicholas, the Chester Police showed up just around the time you said they would. But of course, they arrived too late for Tommy, and as much as I tried, I couldn't stop our attackers from taking Sanit. They were horrible and violent men. Fortunately, when the police did arrive, they came in hard, sirens wailing, guns drawn. As soon as the sirens came into range, these thugs grabbed Sanit and left. In their haste, they seemed unconcerned about me. Things may have turned out differently without the interruption."

I shuddered at the prospect of what may have gone down if the cops hadn't arrived when they did.

"But getting back to the point," said Kaitlin. "While the police secured the scene, another group of investigators turned up. They showed me their ID. They claim they're from the Asian Crime Unit in LA. You'll meet their lead investigator, Detective Chen, I'm certain he's still here."

"It's not surprising the ACU are interested," said Greatrex. "Because of the backgrounds of the people involved, this would be right up their street."

"Kaitlin," I began, "Jack is right about the ACU, but I need to ask you, what time did they arrive?"

Kaitlin drew her lips tight. "And there you have it. They showed up less than an hour after the local police."

"Shit," said Greatrex. I agreed. These people already knew that we, or at least Sanit, had escaped up here.

"So, the frail persona?" I asked.

"When the second mob arrived, they talked about taking me down to the police station in Chester. I suspected they wanted to get me out of here as soon as possible," explained Kaitlin.

"But you didn't want to go?" I asked.

"No, I didn't want to leave at all. They would have redirected you to meet me at the police station, and I didn't believe for a second, they would have allowed you two back up here, at least until they'd swept the entire scene. You would have no chance to see for yourselves what went down."

"So, you played the 'I'm in shock' card, I can't leave until my Nicholas arrives?"

"Correct," Kaitlin replied. "It didn't sit well with me, but I owed it to Tommy... and Sanit."

My respect for this woman remained undying, but a bewildering jigsaw puzzle had formed in my brain. "I think it's time we chatted with the Lieutenant and Detective Chen. After that, let's see how much of the scene they'll let us walk through. My bet is we'll do better with the local guy than Chen."

"Agreed," said Greatrex.

We left Kaitlin in the bedroom. She needed to maintain her emotional ruse. To recover too quickly would arouse suspicions. As we stepped into the cabin's main lounge, the room presented like a movie set. Furniture was upturned or ripped with bullet holes. The gunfire had destroyed much of the internal cladding. The general would have quite a bill in fixing all of it. I hoped he had insurance.

Six police officers stood around the room, a mixture of uniformed and plain-clothed. I assumed there would be at least that number, if not more, outside.

"Mr. Sharp, Mr. Greatrex, are you ready to chat?"

"Sure, Lieutenant," I responded.

"Before we begin, I'll introduce you to Detective Chen from the Asian Crime Unit in LA. We decided we'd talk to you together to save you further inconvenience."

A plain-clothes police officer strode toward us. He looked to be of average height, but solid build. The fit type. He clasped my hand in a firm, bordering on dominating, grip. "Samuel Chen, ACU, LA," he said.

"A long way from home, detective," I replied, straight to the point.

"As are you, Mr. Sharp. Now, shall we get started?"

The Lieutenant led us to a dining table near the kitchen, away from the most highly affected areas of the room.

The Lieutenant began, "Mr. Sharp, can you tell me how you and Mr. Greatrex became involved in this situation?"

I explained about the attack on the band behind Platinum Sound and the assault on the band's apartment. He seemed more interested in my reasons for bringing Sanit up to Lake Almanor.

"So you brought Ms. Mali up here to keep her safe?" asked Chen.

I nodded.

"Well, that didn't go too well."

The detective was pissing me off.

"Please continue."

I skipped the bit where Detective Alroy gave me the heads up about being under surveillance but told them about the break-in at my apartment.

"Any idea what they were after?" asked Chen, now taking control of the interview.

"Probably attempting to locate Sanit," I replied.

"And you, Mr. Greatrex. Where do you fit into all of this?"

"Just here to help," Greatrex smiled as he responded.

Twenty minutes later, having repeated the story twice, we

were done. We'd told the Lieutenant and Detective Chen nothing that they didn't either already know or could have easily found out. Perhaps except for the break-in, but that was irrelevant. My trust levels in authority remained severely strained.

"It seems to me, Mr. Sharp, that you might have fared a lot better if you'd just declined your manager's offer of the session at Platinum Studios," observed Chen.

No shit Sherlock. Out loud I replied, "That would be correct, detective."

Lieutenant Sheppard interrupted. "It's amazing that you secured a chartered helicopter in the middle of the night with virtually no notice."

Greatrex explained.

A short time later, after we'd answered a seemingly endless barrage of questions, Chen took control. "Thank you, to both of you. I expect you want to attend to Ms. Reed and perhaps head back to LA. I understand your helicopter is waiting."

Chen leaned back in his chair. I noticed his shoulders relax; we'd been dismissed.

As Greatrex, Kaitlin and I wandered toward the road with one of the uniformed officers from Chester acting as our escort, our eyes darted across the landscape. The glaring daylight brought further clarity to the violence that must have played out the night before. Tommy Dabbs never stood a chance. The sheer physical destruction of the house suggested firepower far greater than he would have expected. I glanced down through the pines to the water's edge. At the land end of the pontoon, the grass and dead pine needles had been trampled. Now that it was light, two members of the CPD forensic team were locating and bagging multitudes of shell casings. They kept us some distance from the key areas under investigation.

When our officer-minder stepped away to talk to a colleague, I asked Greatrex, "What do you reckon?"

"At least eight intruders. They came by boat. That's why the police didn't pass them on their way up here."

"If they showed up by boat, why didn't Tommy hear them?" I questioned. "You know he's got... had, the ears of a wildcat."

"Maybe they rowed, or had one of those silent outboards, the military type. To fool Tommy, I'd put my money on rowing."

"They were professionals," I said.

"They were professionals," agreed Greatrex, "almost like a SWAT team."

As our babysitter guided us to the end of the driveway, his radio crackled. We waited while he listened intently.

"The lieutenant has requested, if you're up to it, that you take a look at each of the deceased's faces. Just in case you recognize any of them. Of course, Ms. Reed, there's no need for you to trouble yourself."

"We're all up for it," said Kaitlin, her shell-shocked crown slipping.

The officer looked surprised, "Oh yes, fine."

As we toured the scene, the officer raised the sheets covering each of the victim's faces. I studied their features and their attire. Neither the big fella, Kaitlin nor I recognized any of them.

As we strolled back up the driveway, I mumbled to Greatrex "Did you notice?"

"Yup. Two in strategic gear and the one further down the drive in a suit."

We still didn't know where they came from. As my fingers

touched the crime scene tape, I crooked my head toward the officer.

"Sorry we couldn't help. Perhaps the dead men carried some identification on them?"

The young police officer hesitated. "No sir, I believe not."

I shrugged and raised the tape. Then, a genuine afterthought. "Officer, not that it matters, but do you remember which team swept the bodies for ID? Was it your team or the ACU people?"

"I'm not really at liberty to say, sir."

"Of course you're not. I apologize for asking. Perhaps I'll call Lieutenant Sheppard when we reach LA."

"Perhaps you should call Detective Chen, sir."

From the grimace on the young police officer's face, it was obvious he realized his error.

Over his shoulder, Greatrex smiled.

Chapter 20

"Nada, nothing, zero."

Detective Michael Alroy's words defied belief.

"Detective, are you telling us that despite your department's efforts, the work of the Asian Crimes Unit, and everybody else involved in this investigation, no one has any idea who took Sanit Mali, Dusit Salae or Ram Chanthora?" I asked. "It's been three weeks."

Jack Greatrex, the detective, and I sat in Alroy's office in the overcrowded Culver City Police Department Headquarters. Alroy looked tired. His face had developed new worry lines, and I suspected his hair was tinged with more gray.

"I'm all too aware of the timeline, Mr. Sharp, but it's as though Ms. Mali, her friends and her abductors have vanished into the ether," responded the detective, his tone edging on testy.

I backed off. "I know you've done everything you can, detective. I'm just getting frustrated three innocent people can disappear, our friend, Tommy Dabbs has been murdered, and no one seems to have any notion who's responsible," I added.

"I get it, Sharp," Alroy responded, "but you need to understand there is a limit to the resources we can put on this case. The ACU have taken the lead on this. What did Chen tell you?"

"Pretty much the same as you," I replied. "He says they've been able to throw some well-connected people in LA's Asian community at the case. Yet, like your team, they've heard nothing."

I paused, Alroy looked like a man who had given his all. I tried the conciliatory approach.

"I get this is frustrating you as well, Alroy. By the way, I've got to tell you, I appreciated the heads up you gave me on the phone that night, the comment about the interstate," I said.

Alroy raised an eyebrow. The move seemed to take some effort. "I wasn't sure you'd pick up on that. People milled all over my office listening in to your call. It pains me to say I had doubts about whom to trust."

"What caused you to have doubts detective?" asked Greatrex.

"Too much had already gone wrong. How were Ms. Mali and her band located at the studio and then later at the apartment? I wondered if your man at ICE gave them up, or someone else? The facts as they stood offered no certainty," Alroy responded.

"Are you sure now?" I asked.

"No, not at all."

The silence grew heavy as we sat there.

I persisted. "Who decided to track my car?"

Alroy leaned back into his chair. "The group acknowledged you were in the thick of this, so we all agreed. Tracking your vehicle would be productive."

"Did Chen seem keen on the idea?" I inquired.

"Extremely keen. He said it would be a mistake to leave any possibility unpursued."

"What about my apartment?" I asked. "Whose idea was that?"

"It wasn't discussed. Someone must have gone rogue. Plenty of people traipsed in and out of the squad room as we chatted about your involvement. Any one of them may have given the order."

"Did Chen leave the room?" asked Greatrex.

"In all honesty, I can't recall. The place was chaotic, as I said, more traffic than on the interstate." A prolonged sigh indicated the end of Detective Alroy's comments.

We'd achieved nothing. For the previous three weeks, Jack and I had answered hundreds of questions from an endless supply of bureaucrats from a multitude of agencies. It all came to zero... nada.

Jack, Kaitlin, and I made our own inquiries. Sadly, we'd fared no better. Earlier in the week, the conversation with Tommy Dabbs' mother had been gut-wrenching. She couldn't understand why her boy had died. She thought he'd left the gang stuff behind. I told her he had. She understood less. At the time I didn't mention it was my fault Tommy walked back into a world of danger. That would come... later.

I tried one more question for the exhausted Alroy. "Detective, we're aware the ACU team departed for Lake Almanor well ahead of us. Obviously, they'd exposed the location, along with everyone else, by tracking my car. Do we know why they moved early, and the other agencies didn't?"

"No one seemed too perturbed that Ms. Mali traveled with you. We all figured you were trying to keep her safe. Chen held the same view, but he insisted, given what happened, that we could not leave the girl in civilian hands any longer. He volunteered his team to go up there."

"And despite the heart of the investigation being centered in LA, Chen chose personally to go with them?" I asked.

Detective Alroy sat up straight in his chair. "Sharp, it's easy to second guess after the fact. I've probably said way too much already. There remains no proof of any agency acting in a nefarious manner, only a hunch."

"But the bad guys found out about the cabin," I pointed out.

"True, but they may have found out the location simply by following you up there. Perhaps you lost one tail but didn't see a second. I'm sorry about your friends, but we need to expect the worst, I'm afraid." Alroy stared me straight in the eye, "I think it best you two go now, and move on with your lives."

There are different ways of moving on. As Greatrex and I got up to leave, I presumed Alroy thought he'd seen the last of us. I remained certain the big fella and I would move forward, but in a way that would cause Detective Samuel Chen some severe angst.

Chapter 21

As we headed down Hollywood Boulevard, discussing possible tactics to find out more about Chen and his crew, Greatrex asked me, "What was the name of Sanit's band?"

"When Kamon was in the group, they recorded and performed as 'Kha Cring. I believe they kept the name," I replied.

"Do a U-turn."

"I'm yours to obey, but why?" I waited for a bus to pass before hauling down on the wheel, crossing both lanes and heading back the way we'd come.

"Over there," said Greatrex, pointing to an array of posters on an aging brick wall.

I pulled the car over. We jumped out, zigzagging across the traffic to the opposite side of the road. Amongst the kaleidoscope of colors and exotic band names covering the wall, one caught our eye.

THE CLOUDS FESTIVAL PRESENT:

There was a list of bands. The group listed second from the top was the point of interest.

KHA CRING

"Good catch seeing that from the car," I said, "but it's meaning-less. The festival is only a few days from now. Sanit and the boys would have been booked long before they disappeared. All the publicity would have been committed to print months ago as well."

Greatrex shrugged his shoulders. "Yeah, you've got to be right. I suppose it's just a sad reminder of what might have been. Damn."

We crossed back over the busy road and continued our journey.

"You know two people can't really stake out a whole LA crime unit," I said. "They're professionals. They'd be onto us in a flash."

"Yeah, but equally we can't just barge in and interrogate Chen. There has to be some other way."

"Let's continue this conversation at Medina's. I told Kaitlin we'd meet there after we finished with Alroy."

Medina's was our bar, my bar. I'd played there many times. Kenny Medina, the bar's owner, was like an uncle to me. He gave me my first break as a professional musician and was a fountain of knowledge regarding the local music industry. Too bad he couldn't help us with the cops.

It was too early for any live music, but some cool contem-porary soul playing through the venue's sound system set a chilled ambience. Behind the bar, Kenny looked up with an inviting smile as his 'I've seen too much of life' face crinkled in the dim light. He nodded toward one of the private booths. Kaitlin was sitting there, waiting.

"How'd it go?" she asked before we even sat down.

"Not so good," I replied, before telling her everything about the meeting with Alroy.

119

"So, everyone's given up. That's it? Sanit, Dusit and Ram are missing, Tommy is dead, and no one gives a shit?" Kaitlin took a long time to fire up, but when she did, she was difficult to stop.

"The authorities may wind down," I said, "but we're not."

"We've got our eyes on Chen and the ACU," added Greatrex.

"Somewhere there is a dark horse, a rogue group behind this. I reckon Detective Chen knows a lot more than he's letting on," I said. "He's got the background knowledge, he arrived at Lake Almanor too quickly for my liking, and the way he and his unit conducted themselves up there just doesn't sit right."

We sat there soaking in the music, sipping the drinks Kenny had provided, and enjoying the company of the blues and soul greats whose pictures lined the bar's walls.

Above the bar, a television screened black and white footage of classic soul legends. The sound was down, but Kenny loved the old clips. They interspersed the footage with shows from a small-time community television station that supported local music. I always tried to sit with my back to the screen, I found it distracting. Greatrex usually sat facing it. That man never had enough screen time.

"How about we spend a few hours hanging out the front of the unit where the ACU is based," I suggested, "maybe pickup Chen and a couple of others, see where they lead us."

"It sure beats doing nothing," agreed Kaitlin. "What do you think, Jack?"

Greatrex didn't respond, his eyes focusing on the television.

"Jack, what do you reckon?" I tried. "Do we..."

"Holy freakin' shit, holy totally freakin' shit." The big fella pointed to the TV as he spoke.

Kaitlin and I swung around. If simultaneous jaw-dropping

was a sport, we would both have made the Olympic team. Floodlit against an appropriately dark studio background, sat Sanit Mali. She was being interviewed. A banner scrolled across the bottom of the screen. It read:

Sanit Mali and Kha Cring appearing next week at the Clouds Festival.

Greatrex jumped toward the bar, "Kenny, turn it up, please, now!"

I was just behind him, but a little more circumspect. "Jack, this will be a pre-recorded interview. It was probably taped months ago."

By the time we got there, Kenny had turned the sound up, but the interview had already finished. They ran some old footage of Sanit's band.

"Jack, Nicholas is right, that interview may have been recorded at any time. We know Sanit is not playing anywhere." Katlin Reed, the voice of reason.

Greatrex wasn't listening. He'd dug his cell out of his jeans, instantly lost to us as he flicked through several screens and sites. Two minutes later held the phone up.

"Pre-recorded my ass," he said.

I stared at the picture on the small screen. Greatrex had it open on the festival's social media page. There was a picture of Sanit with Dusit and Ram. Under the image, a caption read:

'After losing their good friend and fellow band member Sonitha (Sonny) Saetang, Sanit Mali, Dusit Salae and Ram Chanthora, better known as Kha Cring, will perform in Sonny's memory at the Clouds Music and Arts Festival at the Los Angeles State Park next

week. Mali has stated, "After Sonny's loss, we've taken the band in a new direction. We want to celebrate the future, rather than get caught up in old-world politics." Tickets are available at the usual places.

Greatrex stared at me.

I looked back down at the screen. The post was dated today. "Holy freakin' shit," I said.

Chapter 22

Greatrex and I tore down the Santa Monica Freeway toward East Los Angeles, and the television station. We'd left Kaitlin back at the bar with Kenny. They were busily making calls to people within the industry, trying to find out what was going on.

"This is ridiculous on so many levels," I said. "How does Sanit suddenly reappear after being kidnapped by a group of murdering thugs? Even more incredible, she reappears to perform at a public concert."

"There's a lot happening here that we're not understanding. I know there's only a slight chance she's still at the station, but it's the only lead we've had for three weeks. We have to try," replied the big fella.

I guided the car off the freeway then left down South Central Avenue.

"When we get there, you go in the front, stay at reception. I'll see if there's any sort of back entrance. Call me as soon as you've ascertained if she's still in the building," I said.

"Got it."

We pulled up outside the station five minutes later. Even from the outside, you could tell the place lacked the pizzazz of a state-of-the-art broadcasting facility. Street murals covered the building's exterior walls, while the grimy windows facing the street hid behind thick steel bars. Not very corporate. A single security guard stood at the door. Greatrex walked straight up to him while I lingered. Once their conversation began, I hightailed down an alleyway that ran beside the building. Midway down the lane, a six-foot metal security fence with a padlocked gate stood between me and what appeared to be the facility's rear entrance. I clambered over.

My gut told me this was a waste of time, but we had to try.

A couple of stationary cars lined the narrow laneway, but I was focused on the doorway. As I approached the entrance, I glanced more closely at the vehicles parked out front. My nerves instantly snapped tight as a guitar string. I hadn't recognized it from a distance, but the dark gray SUV standing near the facility's back steps looked awfully familiar. I'd spent a lot of time looking at one just like it in my rear vision mirror three weeks earlier.

After checking the SUV was empty, I covered the remaining two yards toward the building's back door and pushed. The locked door didn't budge. I stepped back, searching up, down and either side of the entrance. There was no other way in. I would have to wait.

Waiting didn't take long. I'd just stepped back behind a vehicle when the station door opened. An enormous man, of Asian descent, came out first. The bulge in his coat betrayed a concealed weapon. He looked up and down the alley, his eyes glancing over the roof of the car that hid me. He paused for a minute before returning inside.

Fifteen seconds later, he strode back into the alley. A tiny figure followed. Shoulders slumping as she dragged her feet, Sanit appeared exhausted. From the downcast set of her face,

I knew she wasn't in a happy place. A second man stepped out behind her. I recognized him immediately. We'd met when I held a fake gun to his head at Universal Studios.

I strained to hear their conversation.

"Let's just get the hell out of here," said the man leading the way to the SUV.

He yanked the driver's door open. As he did, the second man led Sanit around the vehicle. He pulled open the rear passenger door before shoving her inside. Judging from her lackadaisical body language, she seemed reluctant.

"Stay there and be quiet," commanded thug number two.

I had no time to consider my options. Act or don't act.

I leaped forward over the hood of the car, toward the man behind Sanit. I wrapped both arms around his neck, pulling him away from his vehicle and onto the roadway. As his head hit the asphalt, I stomped forcefully on the side of his face. Unfair but effective.

It took little imagination to predict how the driver of the SUV would react. He had his gun half out of his jacket as he swiveled toward the back door. To his credit, he almost had me. Two seconds slower and I would have faced a bullet straight between the eyes. As it panned out, I managed to launch myself onto the front seat and grab the man's right wrist. Using the momentum he'd created to pull his weapon out, I smashed his hand against the car's windscreen. Three hard thrusts against the glass loosened his grip before he changed tactics.

It may not have been a bullet, but the force of his headbutt on my forehead sent me reeling onto the rear seat. Fortunately, as he made the move, he'd dropped the gun. The man reached down to the floor to search for the weapon just as I lunged back toward him. Slightly dazed and extremely desperate, my right arm found his neck and clasped it tight as I delivered half a dozen blows to his temple. Somewhere between numbers five and six, he collapsed in a stunned heap.

Still kneeling on the rear seat, I swung around to Sanit. She cowered into the corner, once again displaying the familiar body language of curling her shoulders forward and shrinking in on herself. I understood, but didn't have time to deal with it.

"Sanit, I'm glad as hell that you're all right, but what is going on here?" I sounded angry and impatient because I was. The singer didn't seem at all relieved that I'd come to rescue her.

"Nicholas…, you shouldn't have come, you've just made things worse."

"What do you mean made things worse? I'm here to bloody save you," I said.

"You can't help me Nicholas, there is more at stake than you realize," she replied.

"I realize my friend Tommy Dabbs is dead, and he died trying to protect you from these bastards, and now you're saying there's no point helping you." Nicholas Sharp, man without patience.

As was her way, Sanit found her strength. "Nicholas, you must go, now."

"You should have listened to her," came the threatening voice behind me.

Shit. I turned to see an old acquaintance, the other thug from Universal. Once more, he pointed a Mini Draco AK-47 semi-automatic pistol directly at my face. Before I could utter a word or react, he'd taken a step forward, flipped the Draco, and slammed the butt into my forehead.

At least I assumed that's what happened, I didn't really know, because I'd departed the conscious world.

Chapter 23

"Nicholas, Nicholas… come on… are you all right?"

Between the spasms of pain exploding through my head, I attempted to open my eyes. All I could make out was a dark shadow hovering above me.

"Nicholas… can you hear me?"

I recognized the voice… from somewhere. Slowly, my consciousness reclaimed the black swamp that had enveloped the place where my thoughts used to live.

"Jack?"

"At freakin' last. How do you feel?"

"Did someone hit me with a baseball bat?" I replied. Not a bad retort for a semi-conscious man. Then I passed out again.

"Nicholas?"

My eyes opened. "Help me sit up."

"Are you sure?" Greatrex sounded worried.

"I need to sit up."

I sensed Greatrex's big hand behind me, as he launched me into a sitting position. Instantaneously, my head throbbed in pulsating waves of nausea. Like a crushing vice. Enough. I looked around. The gray SUV had disappeared, and with it Sanit Mali.

"How long?" I asked.

"When they told me Sanit and her 'entourage' planned on leaving through the rear door, I headed around to the alleyway to join you. The guard was going to open the gate anyway, to let the visitors out. Before we even made it to the fence, the SUV broke through it and sped off to the north. They almost took us out in the process. Then we saw you lying here."

My senses gradually returned. "Sorry, I suppose you expected the worst."

"Sure did, good to have you back," replied the big fella, the relief in his voice genuine. We'll get you to a hospital, you need checking out."

"I'll be fine, just give me a couple of minutes," I responded.

"Stubborn bastard."

"Thanks, I missed you too."

The cell phone in my pocket buzzed. I pulled it out and passed it to Greatrex.

"Yeah...."

Five minutes later, we were on our way back to my place. Kaitlin planned to meet us there. She'd told Jack she had some news. After providing the confused guard with our contact details, Greatrex drove.

Kaitlin paced impatiently across my recently repaired front doorway as we dragged ourselves up the stairs. "You look dreadful," she said. "We need to get you to a hospital."

"Been there, done that," replied Greatrex. "He won't go."

"Nicholas?" she scolded, ever the stern mother type.

"They'll just tell me to rest. All I need is a good lie down," I replied.

"Well, that shows you're not thinking straight," began Greatrex. "You know as well as I do that they'd monitor you overnight but discourage you from sleeping until they ascertain the severity of the concussion."

I tried to give him my best 'oh, shut up' look. It earned me a temporary reprieve.

"Let's go inside," said Kaitlin.

A suitable amount of Tylenol later, Greatrex and I sat in my lounge room, listening to Kaitlin's story. I'd recounted mine as best I could.

"So Kenny and I did some phoning around. Kha Cring had been on the original bill for the Clouds Festival. The organizers removed them when the news of Sonny's death broke. The disappearance of Sanit, Ram, and Dusit confirmed the decision. The poster you two saw preceded those events."

I offered Greatrex a pathetic smile of smug self-satisfaction. He ignored it.

Kaitlin continued. "I managed to get hold of the stage manager at the festival, Bear Larkin. He's an old friend, we've worked together before."

I nodded. The LA music industry can be small, if not downright claustrophobic.

"Bear told me that the festival organizers received a call directly from Sanit yesterday. She told them they were back and ready to perform. Of course, the organizers offered no argument. Because of their disappearance, Kha Cring have been all over the news recently."

"And all publicity is good publicity in this business," added Greatrex.

"Exactly," said Kaitlin.

"So, if the festival people were informed the band had returned, why didn't the authorities react? They would have a load of questions that needed answering. Besides, I would

130

have figured that if the authorities were in the picture, Alroy would have told us. And of course, why didn't Sanit contact us?"

My head hurt.

"Sanit told the festival organizers that she was cooperating with the authorities, and they'd given her permission to perform," said Kaitlin.

Greatrex chirped in. "And the organizers took that at face value?"

"Of course they did," replied Kaitlin. "Why wouldn't they?"

"What about the television interview, when did they organize that?" I asked.

"They arranged it this morning. It was intended to be pre-taped, but the television crew encountered technical difficulties. In the end, they went live to air, hence the fact they were still at the station when you two arrived. Apparently, the festival publicists pressed to broadcast live because they wanted to get word out ASAP that Kha Cring had returned to the bill. Sanit pushed the case further, telling them she wanted to let people know they were okay, and would be promoting a new message."

"You mean all that bullshit about celebrating the future and letting go of politics?" said Greatrex.

"I assume so," Kaitlin answered.

"As much as I want everything to be okay, none of this rings true," I interjected. "Number one, in our brief time together before I was knocked out, Sanit said there was more at stake than I realized and that my presence made things worse. Number two, I don't believe for one second that after all they've been through, Sanit, Dusit and Ram would cast aside their deeply held political beliefs to promote world peace. The

John Lennon thing just doesn't sit."

"Agreed," said Greatrex.

"So where does that leave us?" asked Kaitlin.

"I want to talk to Alroy and Chen. Are they even aware that the band is back and planning on performing? Besides, enemies don't suddenly become your 'entourage' unless something else is going down. Remember, the people who are now 'protecting' Sanit and the boys, are the same people we understand to be responsible for Tommy Dabbs' murder. I wonder if the authorities have information we don't?" I asked.

"Even if they did, will they tell us?" asked the big fella. "I get the impression we're out of the loop as far as they're concerned."

"Well, let's get ourselves right back into that loop, and I know just how to do it."

Chapter 24

"To be honest, I didn't expect to see you again, Mr. Sharp, nor you Mr. Greatrex," said Detective Alroy as he waved us toward the two vacant chairs in his crowded office.

"Life's just full of surprises," I responded. Sarcasm.

"And I've got to say you sprung one hell of a big one on me last night with your news about Ms. Mali and her band," the detective continued.

"You had no idea?" asked Greatrex.

"None."

I leaned forward in my chair. "I presume you've been in contact with Detective Chen?" I asked.

"We had an online task force meeting last night. Each agency involved had a representative there. Chen was there for the ACU," said Alroy.

I looked directly at Alroy, my hands open and upturned, questioning. "And?"

"No one at that meeting claimed to have any knowledge of these young people's return, including Detective Chen."

"To be honest with *you*, Detective," I began, "we're certain now that someone within one of these organizations has been deceitful from the start."

"And your suspicions have fallen on Chen?"

"Yes sir," I replied.

"May I ask why?"

"Essentially, it's for the same reasons we discussed earlier—his team's speedy arrival at Lake Almanor, the way they took responsibility for searching the deceased for ID, and now we've uncovered one more reason," I said.

"Which is?"

"It defies belief that the Asian Crime Unit, a division that keeps tabs on everything remotely illegal that occurs within our Asian American community in Los Angeles, would find out about Kha Cring reappearing from the media… and/or from us. Especially so when they were slap in the middle of an investigation centered on those same people. At the very least, someone in the ACU would monitor the band's social media." I watched the detective react to my words. He seemed unsurprised.

Alroy took a minute before answering. The stern look on his face suggested he was weighing his words carefully.

"There is logic in what you say, Mr. Sharp, and it pains me beyond belief that I must agree with you. For one lawman to lose faith in another is a big step, one that I've been reluctant to take. What you say, however, makes sense. I believe Samuel Chen was aware of the reappearance of your friends well before he admitted." Alroy seemed to tense up. He placed his arms on the desk.

"So?" I attempted to throw him a bone.

"So, I'm afraid this leads me to conclude that Chen may have known the whereabouts of Sanit Mali, Dusit Salae, and Ram Chanthora all along." The detective exhaled deeply. "There you go, I've said it out loud."

"Then we're facing a world of problems," said Greatrex.

"That we are, Mr. Greatrex. The question is, how do we handle them?"

"It's time you went to your superiors and laid all the facts out before them," I said. "Surely they would react appropriately."

"Yes, I'm sure they would if we had all the facts. The problem is, we don't. Everything we've talked about is supposition and theory. If one law enforcement group were to challenge another on that basis alone, the failure would be catastrophic in terms of both results and political fallout." Alroy's fists clenched as he spoke. Even he appeared unhappy with what he was saying.

"So, you'll do nothing?" inquired Greatrex, his voice edgy.

"I'll keep making inquiries and looking under rugs, so to speak, but until we find definitive proof, that's all I can do. That's how the system works."

"Or doesn't work. I'm sorry, Detective, but that's not good enough. Sanit, Dusit and Ram are out there. We can only imagine what coercion is being brought to bear on them. On top of that, I fear for their wellbeing after they perform at the festival." My voice had developed its own edge. I expected more of this man.

"What makes you think they'll be in danger after their performance?"

Greatrex stepped in. "We've discussed this. Obviously, someone or some group from the band's homeland is putting pressure on these kids to stop their political activism through their music."

"You're referring to their statement regarding promoting a positive future rather than rallying a political war cry?" asked the detective.

"Exactly," responded Greatrex. "The problem being, once

135

they've made their statement at the festival, the spell has been broken. But it may only be a temporary break. Once things settle down, if they chose, the band could return to their subversive ways. If we can figure that out, so can the people who are holding them."

"Yes, I see your point. You're assuming, of course, that they are being held and coerced by these people rather than genuinely changing their viewpoint." Alroy looked at Jack as he spoke.

I stepped in. "Leopards don't change their spots. Bob Dylan didn't suddenly start promoting the military machine instead of peace."

Alroy sagged back in his chair, once again staring vacantly into the air, contemplating.

I pushed further. "Detective, until we can definitively establish the identity of these people and stop them, our young friends *are* in and will *remain* in danger. That we suspect this group is being sponsored or at least aided by members of a United States government agency only makes their situation more precarious."

Detective Alroy continued his thoughtful stare. Wheels turning. After a minute or so he looked over to Greatrex, then back to me. Decision made, he calmly nodded his head before speaking. "I've told you how the system works, or as you say doesn't work, at least until we find proof, but I take your point. While there is nothing I can do beyond investigating and pursuing leads, I can certainly support, at least on the side, anyone who may decide to push the situation a little harder. Do you understand what I'm saying?"

I glanced at Greatrex. He offered the slightest of nods.

"Yes sir, I believe we do," I responded. "Can you tell us what type of support might be on offer?"

Alroy spoke slowly and carefully. "While I can't place any departmental resources directly at the disposal of a civilian, no matter how well-intended, I have been known to be a little careless about leaving reports and surveillance summaries lying around. It comes from being overworked, too many cases on the run."

This time we both nodded.

"Even though I'm not meant to, I do take work home with me, I don't enjoy giving up on cases. Accordingly, I keep a spare phone, not my departmental one, nor my registered personal one, to photograph some of these documents for later study." Alroy allowed himself a grin, perhaps a mite sleazy and a tad clichéd, but I suspected he thought John le Carré would be proud.

"Shall I check my own phone for messages when I get home, Detective?" I asked.

"What a good idea," he responded.

As we rose to leave, I allowed myself my own slight grin. I was honestly quite pleased to graduate from Mickey Spillane to John le Carré.

Chapter 25

"Incredible," said Greatrex. "Alroy must have had his suspicions about Chen from early in the game. There's a lot of stuff here."

After forwarding everything I'd received from Alroy directly onto Jack, we sat in my lounge room, scrolling through the files, searching for anything that could help.

"There are some photos of Chen outside Mac's studio at Culver City, and some more across the road from the band's apartment block on La Mirada Avenue," I responded.

None of the photographs were time-stamped, but the accompanying reports covered dates and times.

"According to the report, this first photo places Chen outside the studio a couple of hours ahead of the attack in the back alley. The report with the second photo at the apartment block places him there on the morning of the attack, well before it actually happened." I looked up at Greatrex. "What I don't get is how Alroy suspected Chen and his activities before the incident at the studio even happened."

"A question worth asking," added Greatrex.

Almost right on cue, my cell rang. "Sharp?" It was Alroy. "Yup."

"I assume you've checked your phone," he asked.

"Sure have."

"I also assume you're wondering how I've obtained surveillance footage of Detective Chen before you even called Culver Police to the incident at Platinum Sound?"

"It crossed our minds."

Alroy continued. "I knew that would raise questions, but I wanted you to see what I had, before I explained further."

"Go on," I replied, "I'm putting you on speaker."

Greatrex leaned forward.

"Well, to be honest, it was no coincidence that I headed the police response to Sonny Chanthora's death. Over the last couple of months, there have been several unexplained incidents that involved criminal activity from Asian Americans in our area. We passed most of them on to the Asian Crime Unit. While that pacified my superiors, I grew dissatisfied with the outcomes of some investigations. Where there should have been clean results, many cases remained unsolved."

"So you suspected the ACU people weren't being upfront?" said Greatrex.

"Exactly," replied the detective. "Eventually my suspicions fell on the group led by Samuel Chen. Unfortunately, as I mentioned to you, I had and still have, no verifiable proof."

"What about the images you've sent us?" I inquired.

"All taken by me, off the record. Uncorroborated. Those photos wouldn't hold up in court. I should add that although I acted alone in my side investigation, other cops here at Culver, and at some other stations also held doubts about Chen. But that's all locker room talk."

"Which is why you're happy for us to help?" asked Greatrex.

"The timing of your involvement is perfect. Perhaps now we'll get somewhere," Alroy responded.

Jack and I had worked with the authorities in an 'off the record' capacity before. This had become a road well-traveled.

"Thanks Detective, we'll get back to you," I replied before hanging up.

"The fog gets thicker," said Greatrex.

"It's a dangerous dance, but more so for Sanit, Dusit and Ram than for us."

"Not dangerous— deadly," Greatrex replied, always the optimist.

Five seconds later, my phone rang again. The Doobie's 'Listen to the Music' flooded the room.

"Hey Mac, we were just talking about you, kind of," I answered.

"Nicholas, can you and Jack come down here now? There's been some trouble."

"Are you okay?" I asked. Across from me, Greatrex sat bolt upright in his chair. Must have been my tone.

"Sort of," replied Mac.

"Anita?"

"Fine, she'd left by the time it happened."

"Okay, we're on our way," I replied. "Mac, is this a cop thing? Should we call them?"

"Yes, and no. Just get down here, please."

To save precious minutes, we avoided the rear alleyway and pulled up outside the studio's front entrance. The normally locked door opened easily when I pushed.

We were confronted by mayhem. The comfortable chairs in the foyer had been upended, at least two framed gold records lay smashed on the ground. A large aspidistra, previously perched on a side table between the armchairs, leaned awkwardly on an angle, earth spilling out onto the carpet.

Mac sat on a stool behind the counter, his face resting in his hands. He jumped as the door opened in but settled when he saw us. As he raised his head, the swelling and bloodied features on his face told a painful story.

"Damn it all, are you all right?" My dumbest question of the day. He obviously wasn't.

"Like I said on the phone, I'm basically okay but thank God Anita had gone home. What they would have done to her doesn't bear contemplating," he replied.

"They?" asked Greatrex.

"Two big guys in suits. At first, they were polite. They said they represented Sanit Mali and the rest of Kha Cring. They'd come to pick up the master recordings from their recent sessions, either on tape or hard drive."

"I take it from this mess you didn't just give them up," I observed.

Mac continued. "No, I explained to them I couldn't release the masters until the recording time had been paid for, and that our agreement stated the band planned to finance that themselves."

"How did they respond?" asked Greatrex.

"Well, fine… at first. In fact, they apologized and said they should have mentioned that the band had authorized them to pay the bill. One of them produced a bulging wad of notes."

"And?" I prompted.

"When I told them I still couldn't release the masters to them until each member of the band signed a release, they went bat-shit crazy."

Greatrex had grabbed a wet towel from the tea-room next

to the foyer. He gently dabbed at Mac's wounds.

"So hopefully at that point, you gave them what they wanted?" said the big fella.

I had my doubts.

"Well, no, not really," replied Mac. "I figured they were all bark, no bite. Besides, after what you'd told me about Sanit and the band's disappearance, I thought it might be important to hang on to the songs."

"And that's when they let you have it?" I asked.

Mac slumped his shoulders and looked down, as though ashamed. Greatrex stepped back. Eventually Mac lifted his head, glancing sideways toward me. "They came at me hard and fast, no warning. I reckon they knew how to injure without killing, and they were damn efficient. I'm afraid to say that after a few minutes, I changed my perspective."

"You handed over the masters?" I asked.

"Yes."

"Good," said Greatrex. "No piece of music is worth this." I agreed.

Mac seemed relieved at our response. He almost tried to smile.

"We should call the cops," I announced.

"I don't really see the point of an entire investigation," he answered. "I'd rather let it go if it's all the same to you guys."

"It's okay," I replied. "We've got a friendly cop we're working with. Alroy, you met him the night Sonny was killed. We'll give him the word on the side."

"Now, let's get you to a hospital," said Greatrex.

"Nah, just home to Anita will be fine. I better call her first, or she'll freak out when I walk through the door looking like this."

142

"I'll drive you. Jack can close up here and bring your car home."

Greatrex nodded.

The big fella helped Mac to his feet, and I guided him to the door. Mac stopped as he reached it.

"You two are being real nice about the possibility of that wonderful music being lost, but I should tell you..."

"Tell us what, Mac?"

"Well, I used Studio One to mix the tracks. The big SSL desk is there. These two thugs insisted I take them down to Studio Two, they seemed aware that's where the songs had been recorded and assumed that's where the masters would be."

"What have you done, Mac?" I asked.

For the first time, Mac allowed himself a full smile. The pain caused him to flinch almost immediately.

"The masters were in Studio Two, so that's what I gave them. However, I'd begun mixing off digital copies. They're still sitting there on a hard drive in Studio One."

Greatrex and I grinned simultaneously.

"I'll grab the hard drive," announced Greatrex.

We'd be risking Mac's life needlessly if we left the songs with him.

As Mac and I eased out the front door, I turned to him, "You're something else you know. Two huge Asian thugs bust into your place, beat the shit out of you, and you still don't give them everything they want."

Mac attempted to grin again, before stopping himself. "Nicholas, I said nothing about them being Asian. Those two looked as Caucasian as you and me. From the way they dressed, you'd have figured them for business executives. Hell, that's

143

exactly what I thought, until they attacked me."

"Don't tell me, they wore suits."

"Yeah, just like business people."

"Or federal agents, or cops," I added.

Then I wondered how Mac's attackers knew that Kha Cring had recorded in Studio Two. I'd think about that later.

I should've thought about it then.

Chapter 26

The Clouds Festival pulsed with sound and movement. The vibrant energy of live music resonated across the park, a sea of faces alive in passionate excitement. Angelinos came to the festival to honor cultures from around the globe, a celebration of diversity. You were as likely to see and hear pumped-up folk music from Tibet as Caribbean hip-hop. I'd played there once before, with Patrick Jay Olden on didgeridoo. We'd given his ancient Australian sounds a contemporary spin, performing to an enthusiastic crowd.

Fortunately, Kaitlin had arranged backstage access and parking for us. She'd arrived earlier, after volunteering to help Bear Larkin manage the stage. Who would decline a tour manager of Kaitlin's experience offering her services for free? Like many others, Bear found Kaitlin extremely hard to say no to.

We made our way along North Spring Street until we located the entrance to the backstage area. Once the security people sighted our passes, they waved us through. Greatrex guided our van gently down the flagged-off laneway. There were still plenty of folk strolling across the road, so we nudged the vehicle along at a walking pace. The van had been Greatrex's idea. He'd borrowed it from an industry friend. The signage on each side panel said 'Bang'em Up Fireworks'. Ostensibly, we were there to contribute to the evening's fireworks display. As it was late afternoon now, our timing was perfect.

Of course, we didn't intend to make any contribution to the fireworks, well, not the sort you see in the sky. We'd come for a completely different purpose. We were going to kidnap the members of Kha Cring.

There was no certainty that Sanit, Dusit and Ram would comply with our intentions. After my last encounter with Sanit, the idea of them joining us in a voluntary escape seemed unlikely. There were a hundred ways that their government could exert control over the band; threaten their lives, threaten their loved ones back home. Our plan contained more holes than I could count, yet we had to try. And this needed to be a kidnapping, not an invitation. A forced abduction would give the band, and possibly their families, back in Asia, their only chance of any believable deniability of their involvement.

Despite our doubts, it came down to either walking away or removing the band from all contact with anyone else until we could make it safe for them. Walking away was never our thing.

Detective Alroy concurred. Whilst this event was out of his jurisdiction, he assured Greatrex and I that he would be present, unofficially, to provide back-up if things went bad. Alroy was the only law official we'd entrusted with our plan, although plenty of others had made contact over the previous few days, attempting to pump us for information we didn't have. We'd been reminded, in no uncertain terms, by two officious-looking Homeland Security agents, that the death of Tommy Dabbs was a murder investigation with international ramifications, and that the Chester Police department had sought their involvement and that of the LAPD to break the case. No pressure there. We suspected the festival would be crawling with representatives from a variety of agencies trying to gain access to the band members.

Because of our 'trust issues', Greatrex and I decided that wouldn't happen.

Detective Alroy also provided a solution to the problem of where to take Sanit, Dusit and Ram once we ushered them away from the festival. He had a contact in the Bureau of Alcohol, Tobacco, Firearms and Explosives who volunteered the use of a safe house, no questions asked. The place was only available for a couple of days, but we figured that was all we'd need. As much as neither of us wanted another agency involved, we needed somewhere secure to go. The last time we'd attempted to take Sanit off the grid didn't end well.

We reversed the van into a spot close to the stage. It was Greatrex's suggestion that we put ropes and flags around the vehicle, including signs stating: 'Explosives, Do Not Enter'. I thought the idea a touch of genius. No one would block our getaway. It was also unlikely anyone would shoot at a vehicle packed with explosives. Our own little force field.

We sauntered down to the side stage area, showing our passes again, as we entered the roped-off VIP section. Kaitlin met us at the bottom of the steps the performers would use.

"How'd it go?" I asked.

"No problems so far," she replied. "Kha Cring are due on stage ten minutes after sunset. We've been told they won't arrive until just before performance time. Our crew has received instructions on how to set up their gear, so it will be a case of 'walk-on, play, walk-off.'"

As Kaitlin spoke, I leaned forward to catch her words. A

Jamaican reggae group was in full swing on the stage. Over her shoulder, I noticed both the band and the audience swaying to the rhythm, a single entity entranced by the music.

"Has anybody else been asking after them?"

Kaitlin laughed. I liked it when she laughed, but now was not the time to lose focus. "Just about everybody and their dog," she responded. "Some have come up to Bear or me flashing their IDs, saying how important it is that they speak to the band straight away. Others have attempted the undercover route."

Kaitlin chuckled again. "Honestly, as much as I respect law enforcement, someone should give these cops a lesson on how to blend in."

"Spotted them a mile away?" I asked.

"Take a look around, see what you think."

It took me about two minutes to identify three people dressed in 'casual cop clothes'. Their pressed jeans, the informal but too tidy parkers, and the newly purchased band T-shirts gave them away easily. They may as well have worn uniforms.

"I get what you mean," I said.

Greatrex interrupted. "How much does Bear know about what's happened and what we have in mind?"

"He knows a fair bit about the dramas leading up to this, but nothing regarding what we're planning. I didn't want to involve him further. Plausible deniability and all that," she replied.

I laughed. So, it's come to that. A stage manager requiring plausible deniability. Sounded more like the president of the United States than a roadie.

"We'll see for ourselves," I said. "There's nothing else we can do until showtime."

Greatrex nodded. We both turned and walked toward the pumping crowd. I wanted to get a good look at the lay of the land. We needed to identify as many law persons as possible, not to mention any faces we'd recognize from the other end of the spectrum. My mind raced ahead two hours, ticking off all that could go right, and of course the myriad of circumstances that might stop us.

Whatever the result was, when it happened, it would happen fast.

Chapter 27

Darkness had enveloped the sky, but not the crowd. The massive lighting rig surrounding the stage radiated out across the expectant faces. Spotlights danced across the sea of people like searchlights over water. The previous band, an African drumming group, had finished, energy levels were high amongst the audience and the road crew. The crew adjusted the stage, new equipment set up and fold-back monitors checked. I hesitated for a moment as I imagined Tommy Dabbs hunched behind the massive side of stage fold-back desk, ensuring everything was right for the performers. Sadly, it wasn't a sight I'd ever see again.

Within the audience, the darkness brewed tension. Although the stage itself progressively became less frantic as each crew member finished their task and vacated the space, the crowd gradually edged forward in excitement. Amps had been checked, microphone stands set, the performer's drinks placed where they needed to be. Bear Larkin and one of his offsiders stood at the foot of the stage steps, flashlight in hand, ready to guide the next performers safely onto the stage. Kaitlin stepped back into the shadows created by the towers of equipment. Greatrex and I did the same on the grassed area behind the stage.

All eyes searched the stage and the approaches, anticipation building, waiting for the next act to appear: Kha Cring.

I'd just begun to wonder if this would be a no show, literally, when two sets of headlights emerged some distance away. Traveling down the roped-off laneway, the vehicles remained unidentifiable. They tracked much too fast to be safe in this environment; people scurried to get out of their way. When the cars swung around the last bend, the intense glare from the stage lights exposed them. The two dark gray SUVs rolled to a stop.

Greatrex and I remained in the shadows. Now was not the time.

The front doors of each vehicle swung open. Four sizeable men alighted. Even in the reflected light, I identified the familiar bulge in their jackets and their clearly defined Asian features. Two men in parkas emerged from the crowd, approaching the lead men. It looked like they'd produced some sort of identification. The men from the SUVs ignored them, not even glancing at their IDs. After a bit of frantic arm-waving, the drivers of the SUVs strode away. The men in parkas, humiliated, shrunk back into the crowd. These thugs knew no fear.

Simultaneously, the two men on the passenger sides of the SUVs spun around to open the rear doors. As they climbed out of their respective vehicles, Sanit, Dusit and Ram looked around. I read the uncertainty on their faces.

Suddenly there was a huddle. All four men surrounded the members of Kha Cring, as they moved like a giant crab towards the stage steps where Bear and his offsider awaited.

"Ladies and gentlemen, our next act has been referred to as the conscience of Asia. Please give it up for the legendary... Kha Cring."

The crowd erupted. Many wouldn't know the band, but they would have heard the stories. Their enthusiasm exploded into the night.

As Sanit, Dusit and Ram ascended the steps they stared across the mass of people, seemingly in awe of the moment, rabbits caught in a hunter's searchlight. I noted a moment's hesitation on Sanit's face. Then it was gone.

Sanit led the way to center stage, grabbing her microphone before letting out a deep guttural wail that encapsulated pain and beauty into one raw audio sensation. People in the front rows gasped. A stage roadie placed an acoustic guitar around her neck, Sanit made an adjustment to the strap before striking forcefully at the strings. Ram joined in with a gunshot drum fill that boomed across the arena. Sanit let out one more potent cry, and the band's driving rhythm pounded into the darkness.

Kha Cring were away.

It was all I could do to focus my attention on the surrounding environment rather than the intense performance blasting off the stage. Two of the four thugs that had accompanied the band stood at stage level, on either side, out of sight of the audience. Another one stood at the foot of the steps while the fourth stood in front of the cars, guarding their retreat.

I noted some shuffling at the fringes of the roped-off area as people, I presumed cops or agents, positioned themselves. I searched for Chen's face, but didn't see him. Greatrex had moved behind the SUVs, also scanning for familiar faces. He shook his head.

Then my heart broke.

The band had finished their first song. Sanit addressed the audience.

"Good evening and thank you so much for coming."

Rapturous cheers.

"For those who speak our language, you would have recognized our opening song as an expression of hope."

More applause.

"You may know the difficult circumstances our band has faced recently, and the loss of two of our members."

The noise of the crowd descended into an uneasy silence.

"We've been away, in hiding, but we've used this time to reflect, to find out who we are as artists."

A smattering of encouraging applause.

"We stand before you as the new Kha Cring. Two have fallen, but the three of us who remain have decided to move on, free ourselves from the consistent drone of a troubled world."

Back to the silence.

"Please don't misunderstand, we still believe in freedom, and people's natural right to justice, as you do here in America."

Cries of 'go girl', 'you tell 'em', 'we believe in you,' bubbled amongst the warmth of thousands of hands coming together.

Suddenly Sanit appeared lost. Even from my position, I noticed the familiar quiver in her bottom lip as she hesitated. She looked to her right, toward the side of the stage. The largest of the thugs stood there, arms folded. He nodded his head, a sign of expectation.

Sanit cast her gaze further, to the others beside the stage, before eventually glancing down into the grassed area where I remained concealed. The crowd, although originally transfixed by her words, was growing restless.

I stepped out into the light, certain that Sanit saw me. Her eyes locked onto mine like a radar. She shook her head slowly and deliberately, before dropping her gaze to the stage floor. The singer drew a deep breath before looking back up... to the crowd.

"So, my friends, I must tell you. I bring good news. Members of our government have seen fit to communicate with us over the last few weeks. They have assured us that our voices have been heard and our message noted. As I speak to you, there are bills being brought before our parliament and discussed in royal circles. These laws will create a pathway to freedom for our people."

Sanit wavered one last time. Anyone who didn't know her wouldn't notice the change in body language as she tightened her shoulders and rounded them forward, almost trying to curl up around her microphone stand. The little girl in the garden. Suddenly, she appeared to force herself to stand up straight.

"In the spirit of detente, I say to you all, Kha Cring will from now on be celebrating our culture and singing songs of reconciliation and hope. As our country moves forward, we look to the future!"

The sea of humanity in front of the stage burst into rapturous applause, their warm sentiment rolling back through the crowd like an outgoing tide. The stance of the thug on my side seemed to ease.

The shimmering white spotlight encompassed Sanit, like a ray from the heavens. It was difficult to make out the singer's facial expression, yet I stared at her, transfixed. Slowly, a single tear trailed down her cheek.

She thought that she'd guided herself and her bandmates to a safe haven.

I was certain she'd just sentenced them to death.

Chapter 28

The rest of Kha Cring's set was good, but strained. It was almost as though they were going through the motions, while attempting to remove themselves from their own music. Deflated. For three of the most committed musicians I'd ever met, their performance seemed to lack resolve and purpose.

Kaitlin had told us they'd booked the band to play for forty-five minutes. I looked at my watch. If they stuck to their time, five minutes remained. I moved to the area next to the stage steps. Greatrex, who stood at the other end of the waiting area, turned and headed toward the van. Two minutes later, he'd backed it into position behind the two gray SUVs.

I watched the thug who had been minding the cars approach the driver's door of the van. He gesticulated, obviously unhappy with the vehicle blocking their exit. As he gestured toward the front door, the van's side door opened. The thug turned, surprised. He stuck his head in. A second after that, his body went slack before disappearing through the opening. One down.

The band was winding up, reaching the climax of what I assumed would be their last song. Despite their lackluster performance, I could feel the pain in Sanit's voice penetrate the night.

The thug at the bottom of the stage steps turned to face the SUVs. He seemed to squint as he searched for his offsider who'd been babysitting the vehicles. Thirty seconds into his search, he advanced towards the cars.

That was my cue. I trailed behind him as he inspected both SUVs. When he passed the second SUV, he stared at the van. Unlike the first man, this guy's suspicions were already aroused. He hunched forward slightly, reaching inside his jacket pocket with his right hand.

As he reached the van, I charged. Head down with my shoulder taking the lead, the man's spine took the brunt of the impact. Because of his forward-leaning stance, the thug's head became the first part of his body to hit the vehicle. Although seemingly in a daze, he reacted quickly, pivoting around to face me. Before he could complete the move, I tipped forward, wrapped both my hands around his neck and once more slammed his skull hard into the side of the van. I repeated the move twice in quick succession. Then on the fifth contact, the door slid open, and the man fell through the gap. A heavy blow on the rear of his neck from Greatrex, sap in hand, insured the thug was unconscious, and would remain so for some time.

The big fella slipped out, heaving the door closed behind him. I searched the surrounding heads for any kind of reaction. Amongst the noise and excitement, no one had noticed us.

"Thank you so much for all your support, and goodnight," Sanit's words echoed through the night as the band's final chord faded.

We had to act quickly and decisively. We'd figured the thug on the other side of the stage wouldn't leave his post until certain the band had exited toward the SUVs. He wouldn't want to allow them an easy escape route. We thought it most likely he'd walk across in the darkened area, behind the row of backline gear—amps, drums etc., so he wouldn't be visible to the audience. Fortunately, that's exactly what he did.

As the band shuffled offstage toward the steps, the far man made his move. Greatrex, still on ground level, ran around the back of the stage, climbed the scaffolding, and rolled himself between the stage floor and the canvas that formed a backdrop. The far thug would find himself permanently delayed.

Once again it was up to me. I'd moved back into the shadows as the members of Kha Cring descended the stairs. Their minder from this side of the stage followed. It would take a minute before he realized his colleague had failed to join him. As the thug climbed down the stairs, he stared ahead, his face becoming a mask of furrowed lines and concentration. He'd expected his other two offsiders to meet him at the bottom of the stairway.

The thug then glanced behind him, anticipating the arrival of the fourth man. Nothing.

I stood close enough to hear him say "to the cars, now," before he shoved Ram's back. The drummer looked behind him, clearly annoyed. Dusit led the way toward the SUVs. The thug brought up the rear, his eyes scanning, searching. When he noticed the van, he tensed, alert.

Discarding any sense of outward propriety, the thug drew his gun, again jabbing Ram as he pushed the band forward. This time Ram swung around, the anger on his face clear. At the sight of the weapon, Ram stepped back. The thug's gun, now exposed to the lights, glinted like a beacon. Someone in the crowd saw it and screamed.

Then all hell broke loose.

I leaped out of the darkness. My aim was the thug's gun arm.

I missed it completely. He must have sensed the movement as I jumped forward. He pivoted toward me. My only saving grace was that I managed to roll to the side, mid-air, so the shot went wide. I prayed it hadn't caught someone else.

Although safe from the gunshot, I'd landed squarely in harm's way, falling at the thug's feet. He looked down at the same moment I looked up. My eyes glared at the gun as he brought it round to bear. Catching me unawares, he raised his foot before stomping it hard down on my face. The pain jolted through my body like an electric shock. There would be more to come.

I tried to roll away but got caught up in Sanit's feet. I rolled back, simultaneously reaching up for the gun. I heard it fire again but felt nothing. Then I realized why. Ram's hands were clenched around the thug's wrist, forcing him to point the weapon upward.

Opportunity. I scrambled to my feet, crooked my arm, and elbowed the thug in the gut. He grunted, but his stance remained firm. I repeated the action, this time following it with a balled fist across his cheek. Another grunt, but muted.

While the thug held onto the gun, he was a danger. Maintaining his tight grip on the weapon, he slowly forced Ram's arms downward. This guy was strong. I dug deep. In one conjoined movement, I head-butted the gunman while raising my knee to his groin. It may not have been fair, but it worked. The man collapsed to the ground; the gun tumbling from his grasp.

I swiveled round to Sanit and Dusit. "In the van now!"

Sanit looked up at me in bewilderment, her mouth wide open. "Nicholas, you have no idea what you've done."

"Sanit, I can't and won't talk now. Just get in the damn van."

"No, we're not going with you," she replied.

Ahead of her, Dusit nodded his head in agreement.

"We cannot go," he yelled.

My eyes met Ram's. He seemed uncertain.

"Sanit, now," I repeated.

"No."

The authorities would be on us in seconds. There was no time to debate the issue. I bent down, wrapped my fingers around the thug's pistol lying at my feet. As I rose, I pointed it at Sanit.

"The van, now."

Surprise, fear, disbelief. I didn't really care. Sanit stood briefly defiant, before turning and striding off toward the van. By this time, Greatrex was standing there with the rear doors open. He ushered them in.

Nicholas Sharp, exploring a new trade. Professional kidnapper.

Chapter 29

The van lurched forward as Greatrex stepped on the gas. We were still a long way from making this work. The scene we left behind was chaotic. People were running, screaming, and pointing. Gunfire does that, even in LA.

After securing the two unconscious thugs with ropes and gags I climbed back into the passenger seat and put the weapon down beside me. I wouldn't sit there riding shotgun over Sanit, Dusit and Ram all the way to our destination. I'd just wanted to get them in the van and put some distance between us and the festival. I scoured the crowd as we inched forward. All it would take was a couple of cops with guns to step into our path, and the whole thing would be over.

We'd traveled about a hundred yards down the track marked off by the flags when I saw him. Detective Samuel Chen stepped out from the throng, to the right of our vehicle, about thirty yards ahead. He raised his weapon in the shooter's stance.

"Jack," I said.

"Got him."

A split second later, another figure appeared to our left. He was only about ten yards ahead of us. He strode onto the path, far enough in so it would be difficult to pass him. As our headlight beams brushed over his face, I yelled, "It's one of Chen's men, from the ACU. I recognize him from the cabin."

"Change of plan," said Greatrex.

I reached for the weapon on the seat next to me as Jack sped up, aiming directly at the ACU man. The cop looked startled. His gun was already out of its holster, but he hadn't raised it yet.

"He wouldn't shoot a van full of explosives, would he?" I asked. We'd removed the fireworks and anything lethally flammable earlier, just to be safe, but for the sake of our force field, it had been important nobody else knew that.

"I wouldn't think so," replied the big fella.

As Greatrex spoke the cop's gun leveled with the van. In the same instant, Jack veered suddenly left. The front right mirror snapped off as the cop went down.

"He was going to shoot," I said.

"Seemed that way," came Greatrex's terse reply.

Reality chose that moment to slap me in the face. "We've screwed up," I said. "We've given Chen the perfect opportunity. If they were going to kill Sanit, Dusit and Ram after the show, what better excuse than to have them accidentally die in an explosion witnessed by thousands of people."

"Shit," said Greatrex as he steered the van back across the roadway toward Chen. The Detective was in position, pistol raised, his left arm supporting the gun hand. He was ready to fire.

Greatrex accelerated harder, but Chen was still twenty yards distant. I raised my gun. A pointless action. Too many innocents formed a panorama around Chen. One shot from a vehicle on the move could accidentally take cut any of them. As I decided to hold off, the van hit a bump, throwing my arm

161

up in the air. Justification.

Our captives in the back looked on in stupefied silence. We knew the van wouldn't explode, but Chen didn't know that. On the other hand, if he caught the gas tank...

"Get down, right down," I yelled to our reluctant passengers.

Five yards away, I realized we wouldn't make it. The windscreen was about to become a mess of shattered glass and blood, and it would be our blood.

We were close enough to see Chen squeeze the trigger and the smoke appear from his barrel. The shot boomed across the crowd. We both flinched. Yet the windscreen remained intact, as did we.

"He missed," yelled Greatrex.

"Someone must have bumped him," I said. Luck was with us.

By this point, we'd reached Chen's position. He disappeared into the crowd like a phantom. Greatrex centered the vehicle, and we drove on, any moment expecting a storm of bullets to descend upon the van.

They never came.

"What the hell was that all about?" asked Greatrex as we careened onto North Spring Street and headed east.

"Confusion, luck... who knows? I suspect it wasn't our brilliant planning."

"Point taken," said Greatrex.

"Left here, and then right into Pasadena," I instructed.

"Got it."

I turned to the frozen faces perched behind us. "In a minute, we're going to stop and switch vans." I looked at the two bound thugs on the floor beside them. "We'll leave them here, and for all our sakes, don't attract attention. Get into the other vehicle as quickly as you can."

No response.

Greatrex turned left down a narrow lane, and we screeched to a halt behind a black van, similar to ours, but without markings. Jack sprang out of the driver's seat and opened the rear doors.

"Now," I said.

The three of them appeared too disoriented to object. Ram led the way as they clambered toward the back door. Lulled into a false sense of security, I took my eyes off them as I climbed out the passenger door. I shouldn't have.

Ram came stumbling out. He fell against Greatrex, who was holding the door open. The big fella didn't fall, but he stepped backward, attempting to remain upright. Next thing, Dusit vaulted out of the van, pushed past the faltering Greatrex, and ran off down the laneway to the road. I had a choice to make, but less than a second to make it.

Sanit leaped out of the vehicle, taking two steps toward the disappearing Dusit. I grabbed her, half around the shoulder, half around her neck, holding her tight against my body.

"No," I barked.

Greatrex had blocked any escape Ram may have attempted. The drummer accepted the inevitable and remained motionless.

In the distance, the patter of Dusit's retreating footsteps echoed down the road, fading into the growing wail of police sirens.

The big fella looked uncertain, his gaze alternating between Ram and Dusit.

"Leave him," I ordered, "the cops are going to be all over this area within a couple of minutes."

Greatrex grunted, before grabbing Ram's arm and leading him into the black van parked in front of ours. I did the same with Sanit.

No one spoke until we'd cleared North East LA, passed through Highland Park, and hit the 210 out of Pasadena.

"Well, that went well," I said.

"Couldn't be better."

"We're stuffed," I observed.

"Sure are."

At first, I hadn't noticed the sobbing from the cargo bay, but the intensity of Sanit's emotion grew until it was impossible to ignore.

"Sanit..." I began.

"No, Nicholas," she interrupted. "Don't even begin to speak. You have absolutely no idea what you've just done."

"We've just saved your..."

"No... no," she replied. The passing streetlights highlighted the glistening tears streaming down her cheeks. She inhaled deeply, attempting to stop the torrent. "What you two have done, is murder Kamon. I've lost him... again."

Chapter 30

Dazed and confused. The Led Zeppelin song plagued my mind as we headed east. I had no intention of attempting to make sense of Sanit's words until we arrived at the safe house. Until then, her nonsensical utterings would have to remain a mystery. We stayed on the 210 until we were beyond certain no-one followed. At San Dimas, we switched south down the Orange Freeway. We'd taken a long way around, figuring it was better to be sure.

At Pomona, we swung east and joined the San Bernardino Freeway, which would take us most of the way to the Moreno Valley, our destination. Several times along the road, Greatrex pulled off the freeway and slowed to a crawl to expose any tail. There was nothing.

Finally, we turned off the Valley Ranch Road, arriving at the address Alroy had provided. Our headlights lit up the low-set stucco house as we swung around the final bend of the driveway. We already knew a three-acre plot surrounded the building, meaning we should be secure from prying eyes. Even in the darkness, the sparse desert scrub surrounding the home was an obvious barrier to unwelcome visitors.

After parking the car behind the building, Greatrex jumped out of the driver's seat to open the rear doors. He blocked Sanit and Ram's exit from the vehicle until I'd joined him. There'd be no second chances for runaways.

Greatrex then led us to the timber back door.

"In," I commanded before flicking on a light switch.

Suddenly the entire world got more comfortable. A hallway led past a sizable bathroom and utility area before opening up into a spacious split-level lounge. A dining table sat at the upper end of the room, near where we stood. At the opposite end, down three steps, was a couch and two chairs, set around a stone fireplace. Typical Californian desert ranch architecture. Right now, it felt like a palace.

"Alroy has done all right," I observed.

"I'll make some coffee," announced the big fella as he headed to the kitchen adjacent to the dining area.

"You two have a seat," I said to Sanit and Ram, motioning toward the lounge. I checked the locks on the front door and all the windows before I joined them.

"We need to talk," I announced. "None of this is making any sense. But first, you must promise that there will be no more escape attempts." I studied our two guests expectantly.

Eventually Sanit responded. "There is nowhere here for us to run to Nicholas, you have my word."

I looked to Ram. He nodded.

We sat in an uncomfortable silence until Greatrex came over with the drinks. After placing them on the coffee table, he fell into the chair opposite me. Sanit and Ram were together on the couch. From my position, I covered both entrances to the room and most of the windows. Habit.

"What do you want to know?" asked Sanit.

I almost exploded into a thousand expletives, but I didn't. "We need to know everything. Let's start with the comment

166

you made in the van about losing Kamon."

Again, Sanit drifted off into silence. She closed her eyes, traveling with her thoughts to another place.

"Kamon is alive," she whispered. "At least he was a few hours ago... until you two came along."

"What reason could you possibly have for believing this?" I demanded.

"Dusit has spoken with him. Apparently, he wasn't killed the night they attacked the farmhouse. Kamon told Dusit he'd been seriously wounded but survived."

I glanced over to Greatrex, eyebrows raised.

"How did Kamon contact Dusit?" I'd decided to climb down this rabbit hole and have a look around.

"The men who were holding us, the ones you left behind at the festival and in the van, are part of the government-sponsored group who assaulted our apartment in LA.

"Whose government, ours or yours?" I interjected.

"Ours," replied Sanit before continuing. "They took Dusit and Ram into their custody. They told them Kamon had survived, that he'd battled for his life in hospital, and lived."

I glanced over to Ram. "It's true," he said.

"How did Dusit contact Kamon? Phone, Skype, email, social media?" There were a thousand ways for these people to be deceptive.

"He spoke to him on the phone. Kamon was still in hospital. He was weak, but able to talk."

"So, you haven't spoken to him directly, Sanit?" asked Greatrex.

"No."

"Ram?" I interjected.

"No, they took Dusit to another room to have the conversation. He came back shaken but elated."

"Then we only have Dusit's word that Kamon is alive," I concluded.

Sanit sat upright. "Of course, but that's enough. Dusit has been with us for a long time. Almost from the beginning. He is one of us. Why would he lie and break my heart all over again?"

The question of the day.

"All right," I began. "Let's put Kamon aside for the moment. What happened after the attack on the cabin at Lake Almanor? You're aware they killed Tommy Dabbs?"

"Yes Nicholas, and I'm so sorry," said Sanit, her tone laced with genuine empathy. "When they heard the police sirens, the men who attacked us took me to a boat at the bottom of the garden. There were no further gunshots, so I assume Kaitlin is unharmed?"

"Kaitlin is fine," I responded. "In fact, she was side of stage at the concert this evening, in the shadows."

"Thank God for that," she said.

"So where did they take you in the boat?" I pressed.

"We traveled to the other end of the lake. There was a helicopter waiting. They shoved me inside and then brought me back to LA."

"How many in the chopper with you?" asked Greatrex.

"Four, there was room for more."

I grimly realized that Tommy had bravely assured that three men would not be taking up their seats for the return journey.

"Did you recognize any of them?" I inquired.

"Two of them were at the festival tonight, I hadn't come across them before that. I didn't know the others."

Greatrex produced his phone, the burner. He clicked a

couple of links and then held the screen up to Sanit's face. "Do you recognize this man?"

Sanit studied the image carefully. "I'm not sure, it's confusing. That man looks familiar, but I can't be certain."

Greatrex flipped the screen over in my direction. The picture was of Detective Chen. He then showed it to Ram.

The musician just shook his head, "No."

I turned to the big fella, "How did…"

He smiled. "I transferred all the images and info from my phone to the burner, just in case. There's still more data to go through, but I wanted to keep my cell off the grid."

With technology, Greatrex was always one step ahead of me.

"Okay," I said, turning back to Sanit. "let's move forward. When you returned to LA, where did these people take you?"

"I'm not sure. I don't know Los Angeles very well, and they made me lie down on the backseat of the car."

Annoying.

"I can tell you," she continued, "that the helicopter landed at Hollywood Burbank Airport. I saw the signs."

I glanced at Greatrex. That was even more annoying. It meant that we'd taken off in Eddie Small's chopper for Lake Almanor at the same location these thugs landed with Sanit. We would have virtually passed each other in the night.

"What about the house they took you to? Can you describe it?" I asked.

"It was more like a compound than a house," she began. "I'm sure it was in some sort of gated estate because the driver stopped to talk to someone just before we reached it. Although it was very dark, I remember a mass of windows overlooking a pool. Oh, and when we pulled up, we entered an enormous garage, that's when they allowed me to sit up."

169

As though we'd rehearsed it, Greatrex and I looked at each other and spoke in unison, "Echo Park."

Things grew more frustrating by the minute. We'd been so close so often, but there were no prizes for close.

"All right, Ram," I said. Let's hear your side of things.

Ram sat up in his chair and squared his shoulders. "When they broke into the apartment, we had no warning at all. Sanit only escaped because she'd been down at the local shops. When she returned to the building and saw what was happening, she turned and ran."

Sanit nodded in agreement.

Ram continued. "They shot up the place something shocking, I didn't understand why, because we didn't resist. I copped a graze from a bullet on my arm. It bled a bit for a while, but nothing too serious."

That explained the blood on the chair.

"They forced us outside to the two SUVs, and just like Sanit, they instructed us to lie down until we got to our destination. It was the same place, we know that because as Sanit told you, she arrived later."

"Were you and Dusit in the same vehicle the whole time?" I asked.

"No," he replied, "separate vehicles."

"Let's take a break for a few minutes."

I ushered Greatrex off into the kitchen area before whispering, "What do you reckon?"

"Well, at least they're talking."

"I wonder if Sanit figures that with us pulling the band out of the picture, it's now too late for Kamon, so she's decided to cooperate."

Greatrex stared at me, eyes wide open, forehead creased.

"Do you really believe Kamon is alive?"

    "Not for a second," I responded.

    "Me neither, but of course that means…"

    "Yes, it does," I replied flatly.

Chapter 31

We'd checked out the accommodation, freshened up, and microwaved some meals, before reconvening in the lounge for part two. The break had given me an opportunity to think. I needed to be sure I'd ask the right questions.

"Okay," I began, "let's talk about what happened when they held the three of you together, in what we presume to be the Echo Park house. Did you remain there the entire time? Did you go out? Where did you stay within the house?"

Ram responded. "In a basement, it was a fair size, like an apartment. That's where they kept us. We weren't permitted to leave."

"How many guards did you see?" asked the big fella. "Were they always the same faces?"

"Four men stayed," said Sanit, "but others came and left. It seemed like they had an endless supply."

"Did they all appear to be of Asian heritage?" I asked.

"The ones that came into the room, yes, but I sensed that maybe there were others involved who didn't want to be seen. That actually gave us some hope."

"How so?"

"Well, if there were people that didn't want us to see them, perhaps they planned to let us go, eventually."

Smart.

"So when did they tell you what they wanted?" I asked.

Ram spoke, "We'd been there for about a week. They hadn't hurt us, but they hadn't really communicated much either. At the beginning of the second week, they took Dusit away. He told us later they'd removed him to another room upstairs. That's when they told him Kamon was alive, and that Dusit could speak to him."

"Did Dusit explain why they took him upstairs and not Sanit?" asked Greatrex.

"He said they thought I'd be too emotional," said Sanit.

"Okay, and when Dusit returned, he immediately informed you both about Kamon?" I asked.

"Yes, of course, why wouldn't he?" replied Sanit.

Several reasons occurred to me. "So, you'd been there a week, *then* they told you Kamon was alive. Then what?"

"A couple of days after they took Dusit upstairs," said Sanit. "Two of the guards, they seemed to be the leaders, also they were the ones we'd encountered at Universal, sat us down saying we should talk. We felt nervous, scared."

"Too damn right," added Ram.

Sanit continued. "They said we had a choice. We could cooperate or choose not to. Our decision."

"How amenable of them," said Greatrex.

"They said they would require us to perform at the Cloud Festival as we had originally intended. They also said we must renounce, in a way that didn't appear too obvious, all that we stood for. The lead man insisted that we tell the audience that our government had approached us, and we had to acknowledge that they'd made significant inroads towards the freedoms we'd demanded." As Sanit spoke, her tone sounded expressionless and detached.

"They said that any future recordings would have to be approved by their people before release," added Ram. "They told us that our previous work, the recordings we'd made with you Nicholas, would be destroyed."

Sanit crumbled for a moment. "That upset me the most. Those recordings contained Sonny's last performances."

We all took a moment.

"So," I asked, "what alternatives did they offer, regarding your cooperation?"

"They were very clear about that," said Sanit. "They claimed that if we did as requested, they would allow us to go free after the festival. They said they would keep Kamon in their custody for an extended period to ensure our continued cooperation."

"And the alternative?" asked Greatrex.

Ram answered, his voice slow and deliberate. "They stated that if we chose not to cooperate, Kamon would be killed immediately. If we continued to be unhelpful, they said the three of us would join him." Ram paused for a second, his gaze wandering between Greatrex, Sanit and me. "They made a point of saying that we needed to take them at their word, and not to forget that Sonny had already paid a steep price for our actions. Like it was our fault he died."

As Ram spoke, I'd been watching Sanit. She sat upright, staring ahead, her eyes fixed on an impenetrable point somewhere in the distance. Gone.

An uncomfortable silence, a subzero wind.

"Sanit, Ram, I'm sorry to be the one to do this, but someone has to present the cold hard facts." Sanit turned toward me. I had their attention.

"First, Kamon is dead. Sanit, you saw him die with your

own eyes, you felt him die."

"Don't say that," she replied, her voice a monotone.

I continued, "You don't want me to be right, but in your heart you know I am. Second, these people never had any intention of letting you live after your performance at the Cloud Festival. Once you fulfilled their needs, they'd have murdered you within days if not hours of the show."

Ram responded, "You can't be certain..."

"Third," I interrupted, Dusit Salae has totally betrayed you. He never spoke to Kamon on the phone, but he needed you to think he had. This man is not your friend, I doubt that he ever was.

Sanit looked up, shaking her head.

"Think about it Sanit, you said that Dusit had been with you, almost from the beginning. I'll bet that his predecessor, as upsetting as it must have been, met with some ghastly unfortunate accident." I hated doing this, but my choices were limited.

Sanit maintained her stare, her head still shaking. Tears trickled down each cheek. Finally, she crumpled backward, raising her knees, collapsing into the deep cushions around her. The ten-year-old in the garden, making sense of the impossible.

Ram looked up. "Before Dusit joined the band Chaiya Jiang was our bass player. We'd known him since school."

"How did he die?" I asked.

Sanit spoke, her voice stilted and remote. "Killed in a car accident, knocked over by a hit-and-run driver. The police found the vehicle but never caught the man driving it."

Sanit stood. Although unsteady on her feet, she marshaled herself, traversed the steps, and shuffled to the bathroom door.

Gripping the handle as support, she swiveled her head toward us; her face a distorted mask of pain.

"Nicholas, you must kill these monsters."

The bathroom door closed behind her. The three of us sat in stony silence as the sound of Sanit vomiting resonated around the room.

Greatrex and I sat alone in the lounge. Sanit and Ram had gone to their bedrooms to get some sleep. With their world collapsed, I doubted they'd rest easy.

"There are just too many forces colliding in too many ways," said Greatrex.

"I agree," I replied, "So let's break them down."

"The timing bothers me," said Greatrex. "Kha Cring have been together for years, they've been vocal critics of their government all that time. Why have their authorities acted now, and why send a team halfway across the world to take care of some protest musicians?"

"Consider John Lennon," I replied. "Look at the lengths the US Government took, attempting to have him deported because he spoke out against them. If he hadn't fought them every inch of the way, he'd have been sent back to England."

"And possibly still be alive," added Greatrex.

That had never occurred to me. That Lennon's success in the fight for his democratic rights may have inadvertently cost him his life didn't bear thinking about.

"Yes," I agreed sadly, "but it illustrates the fear governments have when popular musicians crusade against them. As regards the timing, I can explain that. The unrest in Kha Cring's homeland has only increased since they left, particularly amongst the country's young people. While the band reached

176

a level of popularity when they lived there, Sanit told me their profile quadrupled when they left. They're now all over social media as the poster boys and girls for democratic change."

"The power of an uncensored voice in exile," observed Greatrex.

"Exactly." I continued. "We suspected Chen to be the manipulator behind all of this, he seems to be everywhere. If we were uncertain about him before, Alroy's file on him leaves little doubt. But what do we know about the man and his connections throughout Asia? Are there blood ties? Is it money? Politics? Something else?"

I momentarily wondered if Chen was a villain or a victim. If the forces at play here could exert such pressure on the members of Kha Cring, surely they could do the same to an LA cop. We dealt with power here. Ruthless unmitigated evil. It frightened me how few answers we really had.

"Is Chen's entire squad involved, or a chosen few?" Greatrex asked. "Up at the cabin he had a team with him, and he certainly didn't operate alone at the festival."

"We need to know more. We need to understand if it's just Chen working with a foreign government, or is there other US agency involvement?" I said. "The general had confidence in his man at ICE, but word of the band's location still got out."

Greatrex stood up and paced across the unlit fireplace. From the look on his face, I knew better than to interrupt his processes.

"I reckon we've got as many facts as we're going to get," he began. "We desperately need to dig into the backgrounds of everyone involved, particularly Samuel Chen. I'd started the process before the festival but became sidetracked by the volume of intel in Alroy's file, God bless him. It also didn't help we'd had an extraction to plan."

"So?" I asked, reasonably certain of the answer.

"This is more than I can do on a single burner phone from here. I need to go back to my place. I have the tech."

"They'll probably be watching your place," I said.

The big fella allowed himself a smug grin. "Don't worry, I can get in and out unnoticed. The question is, what do you reckon about being left on solo guard duty here?"

I figured he already knew the answer but felt bound to ask. "How long do you need?"

"Twenty-four hours. I'll be back this time tomorrow."

"Go," I said.

He went.

Chapter 32

After Greatrex left, I checked the guns. I had the pistol I'd taken from one thug, and my own Heckler and Koch. My gun stayed with me; the confiscated weapon sat on a hall stand by the front door. Foolish perhaps, but I now had complete trust in Sanit and Ram. Besides, I anticipated little need to use the weapons, Alroy had assured us the safe house was way off the grid and only he and his contact were aware of our plans.

Sitting alone by the empty fireplace, I reran the events of the last few weeks over in my mind, looking for any missed signs and trying to piece the puzzle together. I focused on each player, searching for motivation, provocation, anything that would show the extent of the conspiracy behind it all. The trouble with conspiracy theories is that you wind up making the facts that you know, or think you know, fit the theory you've assumed is correct. Sometimes you can end up in completely the wrong place. Although I didn't realize it as I sat there, that's exactly what I was doing.

I began dozing off in between bursts of focus. My thoughts drifted back to Detective Samuel Chen over and over again. It was obvious he was a player for the bad guys, but what was his motivation? Who else was involved? It seemed like there were players outside the ACU implicated, but who the hell were they?

Eventually the need for rest overpowered my will to stay attentive, and I dragged myself off to the bedroom. Even in my drowsy state, I sensed I was missing something, but I didn't know what.

My eyes jolted me awake, assaulted by the first light of a new day. A couple of hours sleep was better than nothing at all. After a quick freshen-up, I checked out the lie of the land outside. On my way out, I poked my head into both Sanit's and Ram's bedrooms. Neither of them stirred. At least our two young musicians had lost their will to run, transitioning the kidnapping into a rescue.

Moreno Valley existed on the outskirts of LA. It was an area where suburbs morphed into desert. As I walked through the front door, the morning sun brushed my skin like a warm hand, a sure sign the day was going to get damn hot. The few acres around the house appeared populated with a sparse array of native trees and shrubs. No one had bothered to landscape the place, nature had done it for them.

I could make out other properties across the countryside, the bright sunlight reflecting off their roofs. Some buildings perched on hillocks, others blended into valleys. A more majestic mountain range framed the distant skyline. All the houses seemed to sit on similarly sized blocks to ours, the space guaranteeing some level of privacy. It was an ideal location for a hideout.

I needed to check further afield, but I didn't want Sanit and Ram waking up to an empty house. By the time I returned indoors, Ram was sitting at the kitchen bench hooking into some cereal.

"Nicholas."

"Hunger got the better of you, Ram?" I asked.

"Man's gotta eat, even if his world is falling apart."

"Is Sanit up?"

"Still sleeping like a child. She needs the rest. This whole thing has really been an emotional rollercoaster for her," he said.

"I know it can't have been easy," I responded. "Jack's gone back to town to do some research and I'm going for a walk, to check out the neighbors. Now don't take this the wrong way, I don't foresee any issues, but there's a pistol by the door."

"No problem," he replied.

"I suppose a peaceful musician like yourself hasn't had much experience with firearms?" I asked.

"Well, maybe not like the peaceful type of musician you seem to be Nicholas, but my Uncle had a farm, I can shoot."

"As I say, I don't expect any issues."

Ram looked up from his cereal bowl and smiled. "Did you expect issues at Lake Almanor?"

"Point taken. Just be careful."

As I strolled down the road, the area unfolded like a relaxing desert oasis. There would be some commuters here, and some lifestylers. Many of the homes appeared deserted, probably only occupied at weekends, so there was little traffic. From time to time an occasional car or pickup cruised by, no one seemed in much of a hurry.

Thirty minutes into my recognizance, I headed back to the house. The stroll had cleared my head and the quietness of the area had gone a long way to reassuring me that all was well in the neighborhood. I'd been backtracking for twenty minutes, my thoughts focused on a decent cup of coffee, when a glint of metal behind a ranch house on the high side of the road caught my eye. No snipers around here, it was just the sun reflecting off the grill of a car parked behind the dwelling. Like a dog that never forgets their training, a Marine scout sniper never seems to take a walk without noticing anything out of place. In the old days, that could mean survival, but not today.

I walked on for half a dozen paces before stopping. Cursing my inability to break habits, I eased my way back six yards for no other reason than to just take a closer look. I gazed up past the house. The metal grill belonged to the front of a large gray SUV.

Bad habit's my ass.

It took a moment for me to process my own stupidity. How many gray SUVs were there in greater LA? Probably tens of thousands. Get a grip, Sharp.

Back at the safe house, Sanit had joined Ram in the lounge room. They were talking earnestly and intensely. I felt for them. They could talk all they liked, but I doubted they would ever make sense of the way they'd been abused and manipulated. What we needed to do was to stop it. Simple.

Sanit looked up as I entered. "Was it wise to let Jack go back to LA, Nicholas?"

"You put that man in the right technological environment and I'd swear he'd have the names and addresses of everyone on the grassy knoll," I replied.

"Grassy knoll?"

"Jack Kennedy, Dallas," interrupted Ram.

"Well, let's hope this situation doesn't become as convoluted

182

as that one," I said. "Either way, I suspect by this evening, if there is something to find out, Greatrex will have found it."

"What do we do in the meantime?" asked Sanit.

"I'm afraid all we can do is wait."

"Nicholas?"

"Yes, Sanit."

"Are you certain that you're right about Dusit? It just doesn't seem possible."

"I'm sorry, but that's one thing I am sure of. The facts lead to no other conclusion. You confirmed it yourself when you told us about Chaiya, your original bassist. His death was neither an accident nor a coincidence." I didn't enjoy pressing the point, but she had to come to terms with reality.

Sanit's face darkened. This journey was hers to make.

"Now I've got a little research to do myself," I announced before marching up to the dining table, pulling out my spare phone and scrolling through the pages Alroy had sent me days earlier. Like Greatrex, things had become so hectic, I'd had to prioritize, and hadn't examined everything the detective provided. I'd transferred the files from Jack's burner to mine, so I remained off the grid.

The hot afternoon sun blazed through the windows, causing the air-conditioning to emit a laborious whine by the time I'd finished going through all the information. Alroy was thorough, his research helpful. The photo's placing Chen in all the wrong places, backed by the surveillance notes showing when he'd been there, left no room for any doubt about his complicity. The one thing that still bothered me was why was Chen doing this? Despite what you see in the movies, cops don't renege on decades of service to the force without good reason. A few thousand dollars, easily earned, just wouldn't do the trick, at least not for a man like Chen.

According to the notes, Samuel Chen's career to this point had been exemplary. Besides several promotions, he'd received two commendation ribbons and the Police Star, no mean feat. Yet I couldn't escape the same persistent question, what would make this man turn? Bottom line, fact are facts. With my own eyes, I'd seen Chen draw and fire on Greatrex and me as we left the Clouds Festival. I supposed I just needed the reassurance of understanding his justification for his actions.

Before we'd left LA, I'd spoken to Alroy on the phone one last time. He'd instructed me to keep everyone safe and just lie low. He'd said Chen's actions at the festival would be enough to bring Alroy's own investigation out into the open. Once his superiors got the wheels turning, he felt the situation would soon be secure enough for Sanit's and Ram's return to LA.

All we had to do was sit and wait. As a sniper, I'd spent half my life sitting and waiting. I didn't like it then, and I sure as hell didn't like it now.

Chapter 33

As I neared the last bend before the safe house, the sun had shifted west, showering the undulating desert landscape in a red-gold hue. I was on my second prowl through the neighborhood. Although late afternoon, it remained hot, stinking hot. Even though I was from LA and used to the heat, I'd decided to cut the sortie short. Frustratingly, I'd felt some sense of relief as I'd reached the ranch house set on the hill and noticed the gray SUV was no longer there. I'd been even more annoyed with myself for ensuring my second walk of the day passed the house to check on it. Aside from feeding my paranoia, the stroll in the fresh air had done me good.

When I'd left, Sanit had appeared more at ease, resting comfortably on the couch. Maybe the downtime had been helpful for us all. I still hadn't a clue about Chen's motivation, but I was caring less about it now, anyway. This would all be over soon.

Then I heard the gunshot.

I surged forward, sprinting toward the corner. The second shot cracked through the valley. It sounded different, lower in pitch. A second weapon. I sprinted faster.

As I approached the bend, I stopped. My revolver was in my right hand, funny because I didn't even remember pulling it out of my belt. As I peered around the corner, my gut imploded. Parked in front of our safe house was a gray SUV. Both passenger side doors were open, two men crouched behind the vehicle, guns drawn. I recognized them both. As I looked on, one man fired over the car's hood toward the house. Immediately afterward, the sound of the second weapon resonated up the street. Both men ducked down.

Somehow Chen's men had found us. At this moment I didn't care how, but I cared about the predicament unfolding before me. It was obvious Ram was good to his word and was defending Sanit and himself. Although I respected his courage, there was no way I was allowing a repeat of what happened at the cabin at Lake Almanor. We'd lost Tommy Dabbs, but I sure as hell wasn't planning on losing Ram in a gunfight as well.

I craned my head, trying to get a view around the house. Assuming the gunshots I'd heard had been the first fired, it was likely there'd be other men, but they may not have taken up position yet. If they came in through the back, Ram wouldn't have a chance.

I raised my gun, steadied my firing arm with my left hand, and discharged two quick rounds. The thug behind the hood slammed forward into the car's side panel, before collapsing to the ground. The second thug seemed to heave over to his right. Although aiming at his center back, I'd hit his right shoulder. Normally that would have still been an effective shot, but the man wheeled round at me. The bastard was left-handed. He got off one shot, which went high, before I put two of my own slugs in his chest.

I bolted down the drive toward the house. "Ram, they'll be coming in the back, you and Sanit get out now."

186

More gunfire, two rounds. I'd made it halfway down the drive when Sanit ran out the front door, Ram appeared a second later, slamming the door shut behind him. As he hit the driveway, he swiveled and fired three more slugs through the wooden door.

"Get up the drive and into their car, get moving," I yelled.

As they passed my position, the front door burst open and a third man came barreling through the doorway clutching his arm. When he saw me, he jumped to his right, behind a veranda post. A fourth guy followed. I presented him with a double-tap to his forehead.

Not waiting any longer, I rushed back along the drive, firing a couple of random shots to cover my retreat. Ram was in the driver's seat of the thug's SUV by the time I made it to the road. Sanit sat next to him. She heaved the rear passenger door open. I dived in as she pulled it closed behind me.

The door's window exploded in a hail of glass half a second later.

"Go," I yelled to Ram, but he didn't need to be told. Two more rounds hit the car's body as Ram thrust the car forward. I chanced a look over the back seat just as another figure appeared around the corner, further up the street. He was some distance away and receding in my view, but standing in the center of the road, the man's features were clear. Detective Samuel Chen looked extremely alarmed. He raised his weapon. I raised mine.

The two gunshots cracked simultaneously. Our vehicle's rear screen shattered. Through the spider's web of glass, I could barely make out a stain of dark red blood expanding over Chen's shirt.

"They'll have another vehicle. Keep moving," I instructed.

Sure enough, five seconds later a second gray SUV rounded the corner behind us.

We had to lose the chase car. Ram had been incredible, but we couldn't count on him to outrun a professional. This was going to be up to me.

I climbed up on the rear bench, steadying my arm on the top of the seat. All my spare ammunition was back at the house. There could be no wasted shots. I lowered my chin onto my arm. The length of my arm and the pistol now formed the basic shape of a rifle barrel. I placed my right eye level with my shoulder, aiming carefully at the grill of the car behind us. I squeezed the trigger and saw the metal on the grill snap out of its frame. That was the safety shot, the equivalent of a sniper hitting the side of a barn at a hundred paces. It wouldn't stop our pursuers straight away, but it would stop them, eventually.

Now came the artistry. I lined up again. This time my aim centered squarely on the driver of the SUV's head. The man wasn't a fool. He began to zigzag, not enough to drastically slow the vehicle's progress, but enough to increase the difficulty of my shot. An erratic hail of bullets assaulted our vehicle, each contact clanging against our metal shell or sending shards of smashed glass across the cabin. Behind us, the SUV's front seat passenger's arm waved wildly out of its open window as he fired. His rounds were frenzied, uncontrolled. Mine wouldn't be.

"Nicholas, they're not giving up!" yelled Sanit.

As my finger squeezed the trigger, I was sent catapulting sideways, smashing against the car door.

"Ram, commentate. Tell me when you're turning left or right, see if you can give me some indication of the degree of each turn." Greatrex would have done that instinctively.

I aimed again, as though I had all the time in the world.

"About to ease left, about thirty degrees, it looks like a straight section coming up, about two hundred yards long." Ram was doing fine.

The SUV behind us swerved back to the middle of the road to take the corner. When he came out of the bend, would he zig-zag right of left? I committed early. I chose right and aimed accordingly. As the car reappeared, the driver lunged slightly to the left. Damn. Then I realized, no, it was just a correction coming out of the bend. He swung his wheel down to the right. I waited two seconds to allow him maximum time at the outer edge of his maneuver before gently squeezing the trigger.

The world seemed to stop for a second. The SUV's windscreen shattered, but the car drove on, straight ahead. I thought I'd missed the driver. Suddenly, in a single move, almost like a slow-motion ballet, the SUV veered sharply further right, its front wheel digging into the dirt gutter at the side of the road. In reaction, the rear of the vehicle spiraled into the air before somersaulting off the tarmac into the desert landscape.

Chapter 34

"Just keep driving Ram, get us to a main road. We can't afford any dead ends," I instructed. I threw my burner phone over the seat into Sanit's lap. "Can you open the maps app? We've got to figure out a plan."

Two clicks later and Sanit guided Ram north, back toward the Columbus Transcontinental Highway. I looked over her shoulder at the screen.

"When you hit Interstate 10, turn right," I instructed.

"Where are we going, Nicholas?" Sanit asked.

"I have no idea, but I reckon we best head into the desert. This car is too messed up not to be noticed in the suburbs." Gun in hand, but hidden well below the car's window line, I turned my gaze to the road behind us. So far, we were in the clear.

Ram swung east on the interstate. I needed time to think, but that wouldn't happen in the back of a bullet-riddled car being chased down by gangsters.

"Ram, when we reach the Twenty-Nine Palms Highway, take a left. Sanit, can you Google motels in the Joshua Tree National Park?" The tone of my voice and the confidence of my instructions painted the picture of a man way more certain than I actually felt.

A few minutes later, Sanit held up the screen. "Which one?"

"Scroll down," I said. "That one."

Sanit stopped at the image of a kitsch, fifties-looking hacienda style hotel. Its map location suggested it was well off the main drag.

"See if you can book us a room," I ordered. "The less time we spend at a reception desk, the better."

It took under an hour to reach the Desert Courtyard Inn. As we pulled into the driveway, the low-slung block buildings blended perfectly with their environment of concrete, rock features, and two wings of aging rooms. The open desert surrounds, punctuated by scattered Joshua trees, faded into the distant horizon. This was as perfect as we were going to get.

"Park under that tree," I said, pointing to a large Joshua well away from reception. "I'll go in and take care of business."

A long, highly worn laminate counter ran most of the width of the reception area. It sat atop a tiled floor that showed signs of being swept clean sometime in the previous few months. An air-conditioner on the wall over the desk raged like a V-eight without a muffler. Behind the counter stood a slender male, age indeterminable. Judging from his unkempt appearance, straggly hair and a face that hadn't seen a razor in two weeks, his attitude was a mite predictable.

"Gotta reservation?"

"Yes, Raymond Redding." It was the first alias that had occurred to me when Sanit had asked what name to use on the booking. I hoped Ray Charles and Otis Redding didn't mind the steal.

"You got a credit card?"

This was a problem, and why we hadn't paid on-line.

"Yeah, I do actually, but…" Before I could finish, the guy displayed the perfect exemplar of the classic 'sleazy grin.'

"Don't tell me. You're out from LA and you don't want your wife knowing you've been here. You wanna pay in cash?"

I did my best impression of an embarrassed man, looking down at the floor, trying to avoid his eyes.

"Gonna cost you more."

"How much more?" I asked.

"Double."

"Yeah, okay," I responded. A beaten adulterer.

I passed over some notes. He dropped the room key onto the counter.

"Twenty-Nine. Past the pool, toward the back," he said. "You can park out front."

"Thanks."

As I walked out the door, I could have sworn he was humming Dock of the Bay. I wondered what he'd think if he saw Ram in the car as well.

The room was ranch-style basic, with heavy wooden beams, minimal plasterboard and an extra supply of cobwebs thrown in. But it was all we needed, one way or another we wouldn't be here long. In the meantime, I had a couple of calls to make.

"What part of the term 'safe house' do you not fully understand?" Once Greatrex knew we were all right, he couldn't help himself. I'd told him the basic order of events, including the appearance of Samuel Chen, but not all the details.

"Yeah, I get it, but at least we got out. Ram did well," I replied.

"I wouldn't mention where you are, even though you're using the spare phone, let's play it safe."

"Sure, but Jack, I'm worried. The more I figure this through, the less sense it makes.

"How so?"

"I don't know how these people found us."

"But?"

"This is the second time we've turned to an outside agency for help, and the second time it's gone pear-shaped."

"You mean the general's man at ICE, and Alroy's contact at the ATF, the one who provided the house?"

"Exactly."

Silence.

"Quite a coincidence," said Greatrex.

"Too much of a coincidence."

More silence, while the big fella considered my words.

"Nicholas, what you've said is the most likely possibility, but it's not the only possibility."

"I know," I responded. "That's what's worrying me."

Chapter 35

Darkness descended over the desert as we prepared to make the most of our simple accommodation. The lumpy couch shoved against the wall opposite the lumpy bed looked like it had my name on it. We'd arranged for some tortillas and tacos to be delivered, paid for in cash. The whole thing felt very Bonnie and Clyde... and Clyde.

Sanit and Ram watched television quietly while I continued to study Alroy's notes. I worked through it all again. My long-held doubts about Chen's motivation burrowed like a tick. For the second time, I'd seen the truth with my own eyes. Chen had been there at the Moreno Valley property. That fact alone sealed the deal regarding his guilt. I supposed the problem sat with me. After leaving the military, where my role as a sniper scout involved killing on command without question, I'd sworn I would never fire blind again. Chen's actions had forced my hand, so Chen's reason for doing what he did remained a big-ticket item for me.

I'd been trying to get hold of Alroy since we'd arrived at the motel. All I'd got was his message. I'd left the burner's number on his phone, but nothing more. Greatrex headed up this way. As requested, I didn't give him the precise location, but I'd dropped a hint to get him into the area.

"Come as you are," I'd said, "we're near the Sonic Highway."

He'd responded with a classic Greatrex grunt and a wry laugh. He got it. 'Come as you are' meant Nirvana/Dave Grohl, and the sonic highway referred to a recording studio in the desert close to where we'd holed up. The Foo Fighters recorded a song for their Sonic Highway series at that studio. A musician would get the reference, but hopefully not anyone else who may be monitoring our calls.

For a moment I considered the people pursuing us. They wouldn't be certain whether we'd stayed out of town or headed back to LA. Logic would suggest we'd be better off getting out of the area completely and hiding in the camouflage of the large city populace.

Thus far, no one had broken down our door.

I'd been looking through Alroy's surveillance photos for a third time, searching for something, anything, that would give some direction, when the phone rang.

"Sharp?"

"Yes, detective."

"Are you people all right?"

"We're fine thanks, but it didn't go well."

"I know, my man filled me in."

"Your man?"

"Yes, I'm sorry I didn't tell you, but I sent one of my best men up to the valley to keep an eye on you," he said.

"I wish you'd told me," I responded. "It's possible that Chen or the people working with him had your man tailed, that's how they found us. I'd thought the mole may have been your ATF contact. We're certain no one actually followed us up there."

"What you say makes sense, I apologize. I just wanted to

make sure we had your back."

"It turns out we had our own back detective."

"Yeah, I get that… now. My fellow told me you acquitted yourself admirably, Sharp. Haven't lost the old skill set, eh?"

"You do what you need to," I said dryly. "Where's Chen now? Is he alive?"

"He was wounded in the shoulder but not killed. With too many of Chen's people around, my guy couldn't do much.

That meant chances were, once they'd treated him, Chen would still be after us.

"Sharp, I'm also sorry it's been hard to reach me today. I've been locked behind closed doors with my superiors for hours. You'll be pleased to know that as of tomorrow morning, the investigation of Detective Chen and certain members of the Asian Crime Unit will become official. He's done."

Comforting words.

"You're certain this will be all over soon?" I asked.

"Your involvement ends tomorrow. I guarantee that."

"When do you want us to come in?"

Alroy paused before answering, presumably considering the best option. "Can you be here at ten in the morning, my office? And of course, please bring Ms. Mali and Mr. Chanthora with you.

"Can do detective, all we have to do is stay safe until then."

"That shouldn't be a problem. I don't think Chen has any idea how this is about to unfold. Just to be certain, I'll send some men there to watch over your motel. Can you give me the address?"

"Sure thing, thanks" I gave Alroy the address and hung up.

It was almost over.

Chapter 36

I needed to get some sleep, but that wouldn't happen anytime soon. It was past midnight, and I continued to study the files on my cell phone. Something was missing in the puzzle, something just out of reach. I sensed but couldn't identify it, so I kept chasing it down. I'd called Greatrex back and told him not to come up. With doubt's still plaguing me, probably for no good reason, I asked him to go over to Kaitlin's place and stay with her until this was all over.

Sanit and Ram lay fully clothed and asleep on the double bed, hopefully reassured at the safe conclusion that tomorrow would bring. I kept postponing what would certainly be an acrimonious relationship with the lumpy couch and flicked through the digital folders.

The cell vibrated. Greatrex.

"I've been going through everything I can find. You'd be surprised how easy it is to hack into the LAPD's databases," he began.

"I'm all ears." The lumpy couch would have to wait a little longer.

"Well, I've searched all the way through Chen's files, and some of his supervisors. I found all his commendations, plus a stack of positive reviews from his superiors."

"We were aware of that."

"Yeah, we were," Greatrex continued. "What we didn't know, and I'm uncertain whether Alroy knew this either, was that Samuel Chen is one of LAPD's best marksmen. They offered him a job in SWAT, but he turned it down because he wanted to work in the ACU."

Greatrex waited for me to catch up.

"Think about it, Nicholas," he added.

Only a professional marksman can really understand how a shooter at that level works. The precision, the mental preparedness, and above all the complete trust in your training. A marksman's job was more about reacting quickly and decisively to any change in circumstance than a lengthy decision-making process. Some call it the 'third space', only those who could react with a cool, calculated efficiency in the brief space between major events would master the art. Chen possessed that talent, and the training.

"At the festival, Chen missed his shot as us, we'd assumed that someone had bumped him. A pro would allow for that possibility," said Greatrex.

"And at the Valley, outside the house, I got my shot off a millisecond before him. I figured he must have hesitated," I added. Professionals don't…. The logic of it hit me as hard as a kick from a horse. "Chen wasn't trying to kill us; he was looking out for us."

"Got it in one."

The room spun around me. "Jack, I've got to go."

I went back into the files. I'd flicked through all the pictures the big fella had taken at the Echo Park house, but I hadn't gone through them in great detail. Greatrex wouldn't have had a chance to either.

One by one, I scrolled through them. The last few shots featured the late-night visitors. Greatrex said he couldn't make out any faces clearly. The burner phone had a limited capability to manipulate photographs, so I transferred the images over to my actual phone. The device contained a high-quality photo-enhancing app. I was certain that at this point it wouldn't matter if the thugs chasing us tracked our location. I now suspected they already knew where we were. I gave myself five minutes before I'd wake the other two and get the hell out of Dodge.

Of the last batch of images, each one contained figures cast in shadow. I processed each with the app. It took time, too much time. When I got to the final photo, I held out a smidgeon of hope. A beam of light reflected off a large mirror at the back of the room. The light caught a small portion of one of the figure's faces.

I blew the image up, revealing only a larger mass of blurred lines. I tried a sharpening tool to improve the definition. Slightly better. All I had left was a tool that would cut around the image of the figure and let me paste it onto a blank sheet. Maybe then, I'd be able to manipulate the shades and tones in greater detail. Maybe.

My hand tremored slightly as I worked the image. Surprising. That didn't happen often. Manipulating the picture on the phone was difficult. I'd have given anything for a desktop computer or even a laptop. Hell, a tablet would have been better than what I had.

Finally, the image showed some clarity. I lightened and enlarged the shot until the side of the man's face filled the screen. The small amount of light from the mirror had helped. As I adjusted the settings, the man's features sharpened.

I stared silently down at the screen, seeing exactly what I didn't want to see.

Chapter 37

"Sanit, Ram, gather your things, we're leaving," I instructed.

They both stirred.

"What?... what's happening, Nicholas?" Sanit rubbed her eyes as she spoke.

Ram sat up and stared out of the motel window. "What's wrong?"

"There's no time to explain, collect your things. We've got to go," I directed.

To their credit, despite their befuddled state, the two of them reacted quickly.

I'd grabbed the door handle when a loud banging resonated through the room. I looked around, already certain there was no other exit point. The knock became more fervent.

"Just a minute," I yelled. The room's lights were on, so stalling seemed pointless. With no plan in mind, I yanked the door open.

"Sharp, thank God we got here in time. They're on to you." Detective Michael Alroy appeared in the doorway, silhouetted by the muted car park lighting. He stood between two large men in gray suits, one blond, one dark-haired. They each had guns drawn. The man to Alroy's left seemed focused on the parking lot outside, the man on the right stared at me.

"Alroy," I acknowledged.

"Thank God you're here, detective," said Sanit, relief oozing through her voice. "Are you taking us back to LA?"

"I'll get you to a safe place, Ms. Mali, all of you," Alroy assured.

As he marched into the small room, his two men fanned out behind him. The blond stepped over to Ram, who stood beside the bed. The dark-haired man maintained his focus on me.

"Detective Alroy has no intention of taking us anywhere 'safe,'" I announced.

Sanit appeared confused, her eyes darting from Alroy to me, searching for some answer that made sense. Ram just gazed at me, awaiting an explanation.

"If we walk out that door with Alroy and his henchman, we'll be walking to our deaths." I searched Alroy's expression as I spoke. His features drew tight, his lips pressed together.

"What are you talking about, Sharp? We've got your back, we're going to get you out of here," he said.

"I've no doubt you plan to take us somewhere Alroy, but it's not with the intention of keeping us free from harm. It's over." I hoped the resolve in my tone belied the hopelessness I felt at our situation.

Alroy and I glared at each other, our eyes searching, hating. The detective broke first.

"Midson, search Sharp for a weapon," he instructed the dark-haired man. His offsider strode over and patted me down, none too gently. He removed the pistol from my belt and held it up.

"Now Sharp, before you blab any more shit, sit on that couch, hands where I can see them." He waved a hand towards the

202

bed, "You two over there." Nobody resisted, it would have been pointless.

Alroy smiled. It wasn't the reassuring police officer smile I'd seen before. With teeth slightly more exposed, it bordered on a snarl.

"All right smart ass, when did you work it out."

"Too late," I answered. "You were good Alroy, outstanding really, but not perfect."

"Please continue, I can't wait to hear your analysis," he replied. Cordiality had left the building.

I didn't rush my words; I figured the longer we stayed at the motel, at least a partially known location, the more chance we had. I now kicked myself for requesting that Greatrex stay in LA and look after Kaitlin.

I leaned back on the couch, feigning a relaxed attitude that belied my frustration. "Day one, your arrival at Platinum Sound. You faultlessly played the over-worked cop, dealing with a situation recently thrown at him. You asked all the right questions and didn't intrude too much into what was an obviously distressing situation. You must have worked very hard to ensure your assignment to the case."

"You have no proof of that, Sharp, none at all," Alroy responded.

"You're right, I have no proof at all, but I'm correct, aren't I?"

Alroy paused, a leery grin gradually creeping across his features, "You sure are. It wasn't too difficult. I had to swap a couple of shifts, give up a Saturday golf game to coincide with your sessions, all doable."

Smug bastard.

"And the break in our questioning, you left the studio to talk on your phone. The perfect time to place the tracker on my car," I added.

"Touché."

I continued, "I'm guessing you didn't anticipate so much trouble in that alley. You expected it would be easy enough to for your men to take out Sonny; make an example of him. Sorry about that."

"An inconvenience, nothing more."

The monster before me talked about taking an innocent man's life as though he was throwing out the garbage.

"Anyway, go on, Sharp. You're actually doing quite well."

"So, in effect, I led you to the band's apartment."

"Don't flatter yourself Sharp, we had that information. Dusit Salae had provided it already," said the detective.

Sanit perched bolt upright on the bed, I noticed her fists clench at the talk of Dusit. Ram remained outwardly impassive.

"Good point," I said. For Sanit's sake, I wanted him to admit Dusit's involvement. "Why did you make such a big thing about shooting the place up when you already had a man on the inside?" I asked. "Did you have to create a significant show to attract the other agencies?"

"Spot on," Alroy replied. "It was all about the theater. Make a substantial enough mess, and everyone would become overtly involved. We required other agencies' involvement to cover our own tracks. We also needed the ACU to pay attention."

"The ACU," I repeated. "They had an important role, didn't they? Samuel Chen and his men had to end up as the scapegoats. You figured that eventually someone would work out that there were elements working against the case from the inside. You had to deflect." I paused for a second. "The file on Chen was a clever touch. I suppose you'd been preparing it for some time, planning on leaking it when and to whoever you deemed appropriate?"

"And you and your big mate Greatrex fitted the job to perfection." Every word this man spoke increased the risk of me vaulting across the room. My death, however, would be of no help to Sanit and Ram.

"The timing of the assault on the cabin at Lake Almanor has got me a little perplexed. How did you manage that?" I asked.

"It was difficult, but not impossible. Of course, we knew you planned to take Ms. Mali up to Lake Almanor. We'd been monitoring your phone calls before you even met with her at Universal Studios. We thought it would be simpler to dispense with you both at Universal. Her death in a public place would only serve our purposes. Somehow you slithered away, although I must add to your credit, my men said your driving skills rated beyond their expectations."

I didn't reply.

"About the timing. We had a team up at Almanor early, on the other side of the lake. All good men, professionals. Once you'd left, we didn't expect overly much resistance. The man you left behind did quite a capable job."

Alroy was needling at me, trying to get under my skin. It worked.

"His name was Tommy Dabbs. He's a hundred times the man you could ever be Alroy, and he died protecting the people he cared about." I stood up only to have the henchman pound me in the stomach with his balled fist. I collapsed backward.

"And let's not forget your friend Dabbs died because you left him there, Sharp."

A second blow to the gut.

Alroy reached for the door, impatient, he wanted to leave. I wanted to stay.

"What about the ACU?" I asked. "How did you time their appearance at the cabin?"

Alroy paused his movement and smiled. "That arrangement proved more awkward. I gave Chen the heads up about Ms. Mali's location and told him what we suspected would go down. I delayed the information just long enough so he and his team would arrive after our people completed the job. Because of your man's resistance, it became a close-run thing."

"Then there was the warning you gave me on the phone, the bit about 'more traffic here than on an interstate'. Designed to get me to turn around and head back to the lake. The longer you kept me in transit, the less likely I'd be to interfere in your plans," I said.

The smug grin returned. I wanted to damage it. "Yes, that call turned out to be masterful, even if I say so myself. I sent you chasing your tail while we ushered Ms. Mali and Mr. Chanthora off to a safe location."

"The Echo Park house," I responded.

For the first time, Alroy looked surprised.

"We knew about that place, Alroy. Jack Greatrex was monitoring it."

No comment.

Then, finally, "I suppose that's what gave us away then?"

"Yes and no," I replied. "We didn't immediately see any connection between you and the Echo Park location. I guessed that you'd been aware of it from the photos you sent featuring Chen out the front. You set it up well, so with no timestamps on the photographs we had to rely on your fake surveillance reports to figure out who was when and where. So, yes, the

206

house played a part, but it didn't become relevant until much later."

Alroy craned his head forward, keen to hear how we'd twigged to him. Not that it mattered, it was now too late for that information to be of any use.

"Go on," he implored.

"It was the shooting of Chen outside the house in the Moreno Valley that did it. When he appeared, I assumed Chen to be leading the attack on the house, but Greatrex's research changed our point of view."

"How so?"

"Did you know that Samuel Chen is one of the LAPD's best marksmen? They even offered him a position in SWAT. He turned it down to go to the ACU."

"I wasn't aware of that," replied the detective. I could almost see the cogs turning behind his wide eyes. "Sc..."

I cut him off; I wanted this to be my show. "So, his behaviors outside the valley house and at the festival appeared incongruous of those of a professional shooter. It takes one to know one and all that." As I spoke, I felt a tad guilty at my own smugness, but what the hell.

"I see your point, but still you couldn't have been certain?" he asked.

"You're right, we weren't certain about anything, but our belief about Chen being the bad guy dulled. A few minutes ago, I reworked Greatrex's photos at the Echo Park place. That's what exposed you... literally." I chuckled to myself. They'd all understand the joke soon enough. "Do you mind?" I pointed to my phone that the henchman had placed on the table next to the couch when he frisked me.

"Go right ahead."

I turned on the phone and flicked through some screens until I located the last image I'd tweaked. I threw the device to Alroy. He looked down at the screen, seeing a clearly defined image of himself staring straight back.

"Damn," he said to no one in particular. "I'd told them we shouldn't meet there."

The detective, or whatever the hell he was, looked up at me, his eyes burning wide. The snarl had returned. "I guess it doesn't matter either way now, Sharp. Your time, and that of these two naïve fools, has run out."

"Yes, Alroy, it does matter," I replied. It mattered because I'd had enough of his gloating and manipulation, it mattered because this man had murdered too many people and it mattered because I didn't give a shit about the consequences anymore.

I decided to show Michael Alroy just how much it mattered.

Chapter 38

When the three intruders had entered the room, they'd been on full alert, naturally tense. Of course, Sanit, Ram and I had been in the same state. As my story unfolded, there was a certain relaxation in the stance of our captors. Their shoulders slightly more slumped, the guns held a little lower. I guessed that's why parents read their kid's stories at bedtime. Distract their young minds from the stresses of daily life. It was an excellent theory.

A lot would depend on Ram. He was a big guy, and he'd fought well in the back alley at Culver City. He would need to be on the ball now. With my training and experience, I figured I'd have a chance at taking out two men, but in this small space, three would be a reach too far. I tried to catch Ram's eye. I thought I did, but the drummer gave nothing away.

"Enough," said Alroy. "It's time to leave."

As he turned toward the door, I bent forward across the couch, as though I was about to use the armrest to help me stand. Instead of standing, I pressed against the arm, bending both of my own arms. Without warning, I straightened both elbows and pivoted over the couch toward the dark-haired guy. He gasped for air as both my feet pounded him in the gut. Like for like. He doubled over, dropping his gun on the floor. I folded the fingers of my hands together, balled them, and brought them up in a vertical blow that landed on the man's chin, sending him backward across the room. The whole maneuver had taken less than three seconds.

When people get angry, they lash out. That's what I was counting on with Alroy. If his immediate action were to reach for his gun, I was done. I knew I'd upset him. I'd meant to. If he lashed out at me with his hands or feet, I had a chance. A second later, I grimaced as the police officer's boot bludgeoned my right cheek. It was like being hit by a cannonball. The cracking sound from my neck resonated through my brain as my head attempted to leave my shoulders. Momentarily, my vision dimmed, and the room began to spin. Nevertheless, Alroy had offered me an opportunity.

I could only assume Ram was interacting in some manner with his blond guardian. I noted some grunting but didn't have time to look. I rolled on my back just in time to see Alroy's boot shooting toward my face for a second blow. That would be un-survivable. I twisted back on my side, my first thought to locate the dropped weapon. That would bring a rapid end to the situation.

My hands flailed in desperation as Alroy's boot landed forcefully on the rug beside my head. The marine training manual hadn't prepared me for my next move. I wheeled my head back toward Alroy's foot, raised it slightly, and bit hard through his pants. Teeth are an underrated weapon. Michael Alroy screamed as he pulled his leg away.

The world a blur, and a sour taste in my mouth, I risked another search for the gun. Nothing. I sprung to my feet, following Alroy toward the door. His hand was reaching inside his coat. I didn't need to guess what for. I lunged at him, pressing his gun arm against his chest and his body against the door. He snorted and growled as he attempted to push me off.

Suddenly he succeeded, but not by his own strength. Two hands clamped onto my shoulders and yanked me backward. The dark-haired man. This was about to go badly. In a single swift action, I leaned my head forward and flicked it backward with all the force I could muster. Again, my vision darkened. I was going in blind, but if my attacker was close enough... The crack jolted through my skull, as the bone in dark-hair's nose crunched. He exuded a quick groan before his fingers cascaded limply off my shoulders.

In my peripheral vision, I noted Ram and his man grappling beside the bed. Someone's grunts were becoming more desperate. I didn't know whose.

I allowed myself one more scan for the missing gun as I vaulted back toward Alroy. The weapon was sticking barrel out, on the floor, under the side of the couch. Alroy must have seen it too. Now on one knee, he doubled his efforts to reach his own pistol through his tangled coat. Odds were he'd be faster than me.

As my fingers touched the barrel of the weapon, I attempted to spin it around and into my palm. I looked up. Alroy had his police pistol out of his holster and was leveling it at me. I kicked out desperately, the heel of my right foot catching the barrel of Alroy's weapon at the same moment he fired. The shot went high, but he didn't drop the gun.

Leaning forward, I wrapped both arms around the upper thigh of the leg he'd been kneeling on and ripped it toward me. The police officer lost balance and hit the floor, the door behind him swinging open. I was on him in a second, hammering my fists into his head like some sort of manic robot.

Over on the other side of the room, I saw Ram look up. His opposition number lay motionless underneath him. At first glance, Ram looked pleased, then his jaw dropped, and his eyes bulged.

The warm satisfaction of victory stirred within me, just before another crack echoed across the confined space. It was my skull. A tidal wave of pain rolled through my brain. My last conscious thought was of the floor rising to meet my face.

Hello darkness my old friend. No one had told me about the fourth man waiting outside.

Chapter 39

It's a common misconception that when someone gets punched out in a fight, they remain unconscious for hours. Unless there is serious internal damage, it's usually just minutes.

This wasn't the first time someone had knocked me out of late. I was getting damn sick of it.

"Nicholas, Nicholas, can you hear me?" Sound is commonly the initial sensation to awaken.

I opened my eyes, slowly and with effort. Sanit's face perched inches away from mine, her eyebrows narrowed in concern.

"Nicholas, you're back. How do you feel?" she asked.

"Freight train and atomic bomb are the first words that come to mind," I groaned. "How long have I been out?"

"Not long, but long enough." Ram's voice penetrated my increasing consciousness.

The terrible rumbling through my brain and the constant thumping of the side of my head against some immovable object told me circumstances had changed. A couple of seconds later, I realized my mistake. My head banged relentlessly against the unlined metal floor of a van traveling at some speed.

I slid myself upright, pushing up against the van's sidewalls. A difficult task with my hands zip-tied behind my back. Across the van, Sanit and Ram looked to be in the same state. Both appeared unharmed. That is, apart from some serious bruising on Ram's face. He caught me staring at it.

"Yeah, after the extra man came in and took you out, my guy, the blond, gave me a working over. Of course, he waited until they tied my hands before he laid into me."

"Sanit?" I asked.

"I'm fine. We nearly made it Nicholas. You two were incredible back there. If it wasn't for that guy…"

I eased myself up further until I leaned on the wheel arch.

"I'm afraid in this case Sanit, nearly is nowhere near good enough," I replied. "Any notion where they're taking us?"

"None," Ram responded. "Apart from ordering us into the van, they haven't said a word."

"Shut up back there," came a voice from the front of the vehicle. With no dividing partition between the cargo bay and the front seats, blondie and dark-hair's outlines were clearly visible in the passing headlights.

"Wanna come back here and make me?" I suggested.

Dark-hair swung around in the passenger seat. Even in the dim light, the hatred of his stare spoke of his enthusiasm to do just that.

"Where's Alroy?"

"Shut up."

"Where are you taking us?"

"Shut up."

"You won't get away with this."

Laughter. My final cliché wasted.

For over two hours, we bounced about, banging from floor

214

to wall and back again. The number of headlights coming the other way gradually diminished until they disappeared completely. Any fool could figure out our journey would end in some isolated location. That didn't bode well for our future health, although my care factor decreased with each passing mile. My head throbbed like being ground in a vice.

Finally, the van lurched to a stop. Both the men in the front got out, slamming the doors closed behind them. I winced in pain at the sound. The night wind whistled around the van's exterior as we waited, then waited some more.

"Nicholas, does anyone have any idea where we are? Even a vague notion?" asked Sanit. "Jack?"

"He knows we're somewhere in the Joshua Tree National Park, or at least we were. That being said, we could now be anywhere between Joshua Tree and the Mojave, or somewhere else. The only safe assumption we can reach is that judging from the lack of traffic, they didn't head back into LA."

"So what do we do?" Sanit asked, her voice trembling with uncertainty.

I wanted to reassure her, to reassure both of them, but I had nothing. "I can't tell you anything that will make this better," I said, "and I have no plan."

Nicholas Sharp, a calming voice in an emergency.

Another hour elapsed with no sign of human activity. No one seemed concerned for our comfort. What would be the point?

Eventually, without warning, the side door of the vehicle heaved open behind me. I almost somersaulted out into the dirt.

"Out, and on your feet." Blondie.

The chilled desert air ran through me like an icy blade as

we stood gazing into the darkness. The moonlight provided just enough light to make out some sort of structure in the distance. On closer perusal, it appeared to be two structures, symmetrical, each around thirty feet high and seven or eight feet wide. A smattering of smaller buildings surrounded them.

Apart from the building, I saw no sign of life in any direction. If not in the middle of nowhere, we were damn close to it.

"Walk," said dark-hair. I felt a prod in my back to egg me along. If he'd hit me any harder, I'd have been flat on the ground.

As we made our way across the rocky terrain, the buildings loomed above us. They looked deserted, in fact they looked like they'd been deserted for a long time.

"Inside." Prod repeated. Dark-hair may have been angry with me but given half a chance I'd redefine fury for him.

A small battery-powered lamp provided the only light within the space. It revealed four barren walls reaching upward until they receded into the shadows. A figure shrouded in semi-darkness stood in the far corner. He stepped into the flickering glow. Alroy.

"Well, I see you're back in the land of the living Sharp. I assure you you'll only be in that state for a short while."

God, I hated that shit.

"Cut the threats Alroy. We know what you intend."

"Fair enough," the detective shrugged his shoulders. "Make yourselves uncomfortable, you'll be here for a bit longer."

As Alroy spoke, he stepped further out of the shadows. His face appeared puffy and bruised. Signs of recent blood congealed around his nose and mouth. The man would have to have been in some pain. Although good news, I suspected he intended to make it a reciprocal arrangement. Something to look forward to.

"And where exactly is here, Alroy?" I inquired.

After a second's hesitation, he responded. "Chubbuck, California. Population zero, police force zero. No rescue party here. The place used to be a mining settlement." He waved his arm, the consummate host. "This functioned as the old explosives building, but you won't be telling anyone about it." The snarl looked worse in the semi-darkness.

A firm pair of hands shoved me onto the hard concrete floor. The same happened for Ram and Sanit. These men doubtlessly intended to kill us, I just hoped they were professional enough to make it quick and painless.

"We can't go anywhere, Alroy. How about untying us?" I asked.

"In your dreams, Sharp. Do you really think I'd fall for that twice?"

With those words, Alroy marched out of the room. Blondie and dark-hair retreated toward the shadows. Their guns glinted in the half-light, their eyes glowing like Jackals out-waiting their prey.

Chapter 40

"Up, on your feet. You're leaving." Blondie had no morning manners.

As Sanit, Ram and I roused ourselves from what had barely been a sleep at all, I looked out the open doorway. It was still dark.

"What time is it?" asked Sanit.

"Time to get moving," Blondie leered. "You've got a plane to catch."

A plane? Out here? I'd expected the end of a barrel or a shove down a mineshaft. If Alroy was trying to confuse us, he was doing a good job.

We stumbled out into the night. The wind had died slightly, but it remained bitterly cold.

"In the van." I recognized dark-hair's voice. I stepped forward quickly to save him the satisfaction of another prod in the back. Survival.

We clambered in, but with some difficulty. My hands, and I assumed those of the other two, were numb from the cable ties. Even if someone cut them loose, I'd have trouble using them. In a now-familiar pattern, after slamming the side door shut, our two guards climbed into the front seat and sped off into the night. Compared to the relatively smooth road we'd traveled on the day before, this track felt like we were driving over a rock garden. Sanit, Ram and I searched each other's faces for any sign of ideas or optimism. Their blank expressions told a story of hope abandoned.

Thirty minutes later, we pulled to a stop. Same procedure. Blondie and dark-hair shoved us out the side of the van toward another ominous looking structure. The topography here was flat, but in the dim morning light I could make out hills silhouetted in the distance. We seemed to be in some kind of long valley.

As they pushed us forward, the building emerged out of the gloom. It wasn't much more than an oversized tin shed. The enormous sliding door stood wide open and a shaft of light beamed through it, guiding us.

"In."

As we entered the huge shed, my first thought was hangar, but only for relatively small planes. The long metal beams that held up the tin room seemed plagued by surface rust. Even in the artificial light, I made out rusted holes chaotically spread along the walls. There had been no maintenance performed here in years. Presumably empty, several drums marked 'Avgas', lay scattered around the gravel floor.

Predictably, as before, Michael Alroy appeared out of the semi-darkness into the center of the space. He enjoyed a good entrance. I hoped I'd figure a way to provide him with a similarly good but less comfortable exit.

"Abandoned airstrip Alroy, how convenient," I said.

"There's plenty of them around here, facilities leftover from a bygone era. Sadly, there are no lights on the runway. That's why you had to stay over at the mine for a sunrise departure."

"And where the hell are we going?" I asked.

"Think of it as a personal tour, with separate destinations to suit each traveler. In the case of Ms. Mali and Mr. Chanthora, they'll be flown over the border to Mexico. From there, we've arranged an international flight which will repatriate them to their homeland."

Sanit lunged forwards, blondie blocked her. "We're not leaving, no way."

"You're not only going, but I'm coming with you," announced a voice from the shadows. Dusit Salae sidled into view.

Ram's reaction was instant. He let out a primal roar, shoved dark-hair aside, and vaulted toward Dusit. He was mid-air when Alroy stepped to his right, lifted a crowbar I hadn't even noticed in his hand, and brought it down with maximum force on Ram's shoulders and neck. Ram crumpled to the floor.

"Pointless," said Alroy, not a trace of concern in his voice. He swung back to Sanit. "Yes, you'll go, Ms. Mali, and it gets better from there. Your band will perform a concert on your royal family's palace grounds. After your announcement at the Clouds Festival, there was much celebration about your newly gained support of the government. This concert will cement that belief into the culture of the youth, quelling their desire for revolt. The influence modern music has over the younger generations really is amazing."

"You can't make us do it," Sanit said. "We won't play."

"Oh, you'll play," replied Alroy, "because if you don't ten of your followers will be rounded up and shot each day, until you do."

"You wouldn't do that," said Sanit, her voice pleading.

"Maybe I wouldn't, but I won't have to. That's not my role in this affair. I only have to deliver you into the hands of your country's secret service. They'll take care of the rest. It's my understanding they can be quite brutal."

"You're a jerk, Alroy,"

"I'm a survivor Sharp, sadly that's something you're not."

Sanit stood there trembling in anger. This girl had seen so much in her brief life. There was nothing in the playbook that said she possibly deserved this.

"What about Nicholas? Is he coming with us?" she asked.

"No, Sanit," I replied. "I think Alroy has a completely different plan for me." My eyes remained glued to the detective's as I spoke.

"Quite right, Sharp. Not long after we take off, while we're still at a relatively low altitude, you're going to have a change of heart."

"He'd never…." began Sanit before Alroy held up his hand.

"Don't be stupid, child," Alroy interrupted. "This stubborn fool won't betray you, he'll simply leave you."

"Through the side door of the plane at around a thousand feet, I expect."

"Exactly, Sharp."

"You're a monster," yelled Sanit.

"No, Ms. Mali. As mentioned, just a survivor."

I didn't think Alroy had yet revealed all his plans. Sanit and Ram needed to hear what he had in mind.

"And what about after their performance? What if Kha Cring retract what they'd said?" I was certain Alroy would enjoy responding. It was in his nature.

"Well, they could go on killing Kha Cring followers endlessly, but in time, that would become messy and hard to explain. Apparently, the arrangement is that after the band's appearance there will be quite a post-show party. There'll be lots of famous faces and a strong media presence there. Sadly, there will also be a terrorist incident in which all the members of the band, except Mr. Salae, will be killed in an explosion. Rightist militants will be blamed, caught, and executed. In secrecy, of course."

The plan Alroy had outlined was outrageous, but given the circumstances, it seemed feasible. Off the top of my head, I saw no reason these people wouldn't succeed. I also saw no way to stop them.

I glanced behind me. Outside the hanger, the light was growing. Our ride to eternity would arrive soon. I turned back to Alroy.

"Forgive my stupidity," I began. "There is a small chance your plan might work, but the one thing I can't see is what's in it for you, Alroy. How did you get involved in all of this?"

In my experience, wicked men always seemed to feel the need to explain themselves. There may be some deeper psychology behind the pattern, but I really didn't care. Each second we remained on the ground, if not a chance to survive, was at the very least a second longer to live. Alroy proved my point.

"It's actually not that complicated Sharp. Like many in law enforcement, my politics have always leaned to the right. Something to do with catching criminals then having weak, self-righteous judges give them endless second, third, fourth... whatever, chances, I expect. It turns out several Homeland Security personnel I knew socially, shared my frustrations. Not all, just an elite few who had become disenchanted and were searching for a better way. Let me tell you, there is nobody more dangerous than a disillusioned cop.

Anyway, these agents began making contacts with individuals in other agencies across the country. Some innocent 'professional networking' if you like."

Alroy held his hands up as inverted commas as he said the words. I assumed he was thinking sarcasm; I was thinking Dr. Evil, but this man was no parody.

"As time passed, conversations turned into ideas, ideas into plans. We built powerful relationships. Some of us had contacts with the aforementioned secret service in Ms. Mali and Mr. Chanthora's homeland. It was a meeting of minds, so to speak. Their people didn't want their county going down the same liberal road that the US has traveled. Of course, they had the direct support of their government and royal family to reinforce their views. Not like here. Kha Cring stood for everything these people loathed, and the band's popularity was rising. Fleeing to the states did nothing to hinder that, if anything, it only created greater devotion in their followers."

Alroy tilted his head to one side, as though talking to an infant. I thought he honestly tried to smile, but it came across as a lopsided version of his sneer. In front of us, Ram groaned as he struggled to pick himself up under the watchful eye of blondie and dark-hair. I now assumed them both to be part of Alroy's group of recalcitrant Homeland Security agents. As he rose on one knee, the drummer shook his head and winced; I wasn't sure if it was because of the blow from the crowbar or Alroy's macabre story.

Alroy continued. "We made firm plans to help our Asian colleagues. The rest, as they say, is history."

"So you've done all of this, facilitated these murders and more to come, because of some misguided ideological leaning?" The anger surged within me as I spoke.

"Don't be a fool Sharp, you think too much of me."

Stupefied silence.

223

"I wish I could say that were the case, but there wouldn't be a word of truth in it," he continued. "The ideology may have originally brought us together, and facilitated a few favors and the odd tip-off, but not an operation of this magnitude. Truth be told, ideologically speaking, I don't really give a shit who wins now, either here or overseas." Again, the detective paused, allowing himself a final moment of theater. His face flashed from contorted frustration to self-satisfied joy in no time flat. "I did it for eight million dollars deposited in an offshore account."

The rage in Ram's voice stung deep as he expelled a second dark, guttural scream. Already halfway across the distance between them, he lunged toward Alroy, both hands forming claws ready to wrap around the detective's neck. His speed and strength, now powered by his anger, aimed solely at the destruction of the man before him.

Alroy backed up in surprise, but he wasn't quick enough. Ram's fingers found his throat. I turned to blondie and dark-hair. The latter was pointing his pistol directly at my chest. I had nowhere to go. Ram squeezed Alroy's neck, grunting in determination as the police officer's face turned crimson. A single gunshot rang out across the hangar, its deafening blast amplified by the building's sheet metal walls. Ram faltered but held his grip. Then another boom reverberated through the building. Ram stumbled backward, an expanding splotch of red soaking through his shirt. His eyes stared fixedly to the right of Alroy's shoulder, focusing on the man who'd just shot him.

With words as effortless and cold as I'd ever heard, Dusit Salae lowered his gun and spoke directly to Sanit, "I'm guessing we'll be performing as a duo then."

Chapter 41

Sanit collapsed on the ground, weeping uncontrollably. Who could blame her? I stood frozen on the spot, unable to move without giving dark-hair the chance he sought.

Alroy looked at Dusit, "That wasn't really needed, but thanks."

Dusit shrugged, like he didn't care one way or another. "Let's get the girl on the plane."

Blondie reached down, grabbed Sanit's arm, and dragged her onto her feet. As she rose, the singer turned to Dusit.

"Why Dusit? Why would you do this to us? Did Ram mean nothing to you? Or Sonny? Or Kamon?"

"You're so naïve, Sanit, and Kamon and the others even more so. You were never going to get away with spitting in the face of our government. I tried to stop you, but you had no ears for my words. By the way, yes, it was me. I told the authorities about the location of the farmhouse so they would take Kamon out. I knew he'd end up taking you down with him if he wasn't removed, permanently. After that, I hoped you might give up. I actually thought there may be something between us in the future." For a moment Dusit looked away, avoiding Sanit's stare. "Well, I was the naïve one there, wasn't I?"

As he spoke, Dusit had advanced toward Sanit, his face now

inches from hers, challenging her.

Sanit's features drew tight. Tears still streamed down her cheeks. She was balancing on an emotional cliff. I wondered if she would withdraw, as she had so often before.

Abruptly the little girl in the garden disappeared. The tears faltered, her eyes darkened in anger. She glanced over Dusit's shoulder, seeing Ram laying motionless on the ground, blood pooling around him. In a single movement, she turned back to Dusit and spat in his face.

He recoiled, "Get the bitch out of here."

Alroy laughed.

As we walked out the hangar door, the sun lit the desert landscape. In other circumstances, the sight would be something to behold. In other circumstances…

Unseen in the dark when we arrived, a basic runway stretched the length of the valley floor, running parallel to the shed. It wouldn't land a jet airliner, but for Alroy's purposes it would take any plane he needed.

We'd reached five steps into the open when the sound of a car engine echoed across the terrain. Alroy snapped his head around, as did I. Yet another gray SUV headed toward us. How many did they have at their disposal?

"Excellent," said Alroy. "One more surprise for you Sharp."

The SUV pulled up next to us. The back driver's side door swung open. Another of the indeterminable number of men in dark suits got out. He reached into the vehicle and grabbed at something… or someone. My heart sank as soon as I saw the first strands of flowing blond hair. Kaitlin Reed broke free of the man's grip and stood bolt upright, her hands zip-tied together.

"You bastard Alroy, there was no need," I hissed.

"There was every need. We couldn't leave any 'loose ends' as they say in the movies. We tried to grab your friend Greatrex as well but couldn't track him down. Don't worry about that, we'll get him soon, before he can do us any further damage."

"Don't count on it," I said. It was tempting to tell him that if his men had waited at Kaitlin's place a short time longer, Greatrex would have turned up. For what it was worth, at least the big fella would now presume Kaitlin to be missing as well.

"You all right?" I asked Kaitlin.

"Never better."

As we spoke, a faint hum filtered through the sky. I looked up. In the distance, a glint of metal flashed in the increasing sunlight. The plane, our plane. The one certainty was that none of us should get aboard that aircraft if we wanted to stay alive. The trouble being, I remained devoid of any substantial or even remotely workable plan that would keep us grounded.

We stood waiting, transfixed by the plane as it closed in on us. Eventually the sound of its engines overpowered any conversation, as the aircraft swept down to overfly the runway. Standard procedure on a remote airfield. On its second pass, the plane lined up with the end of the dirt airstrip and gently descended to a touchdown. At the opposite end of the strip, its engines wound down to a quiet chatter before it taxied toward us.

From its shape, it looked to be some sort of Cessna, certainly big enough for all of us. The aircraft was a high wing design, suitable for parachutists. I noted the sliding door on the side of the fuselage, also good for parachutists, although I held little hope that Alroy intended to supply me with one. My gut churned as I thought about Kaitlin being forced out of the plane with me.

We couldn't get on that plane.

As the aircraft stopped, Alroy yelled to his men above the noise of the idling engine, "Get everyone on board, now." He turned to dark-hair. "Check the ties on Sharp's hands are tight, don't give him an inch."

Dark-hair never seemed to tire of causing me pain. He stepped forward, grabbed my wrists and wrenched the zip ties binding my hands behind my back tighter than I would have thought possible. Then he stepped away and prodded me with his gun. With a little luck, that habit would backfire on him.

Alroy stood at the aircraft's side door, beckoning his men along. "Come on now, all aboard," the smug fool was enjoying his moment of victory. Only he was no fool. Without warning, the plane's engine changed in tone. Alroy noticed it as well. He looked up at the pilot. The engine note seemed to change again. In a split second, I realized the variation in mechanical sound had nothing to do with the aircraft at all. I swung around to track the source.

Three black SUVs had reached the edge of the airstrip. Their motors revved stridently as they sped toward us. From their speed, it looked as though they had no intention of slowing until they reached us.

Alroy had also turned around. The manner in which he jumped made it clear these weren't more of his men arriving.

"On the plane, now," he screamed.

Pandemonium broke out.

Sanit stood closest to Alroy and the plane's open door. Blondie shoved her through the entrance. With her hands still tied behind her back, she landed with a thump, face down on the aircraft's floor. Blondie then reached over, grabbed Kaitlin's arm and catapulted her through the opening. Her wrists bound in front of her, she could at least cushion her fall.

"Move it," said Alroy. He was starting to panic.

Right on cue, dark-hair shoved me in the back again. I was expecting it. In one movement, I leaned forward and raised my arms behind my back as high as possible. I then brought them crashing down with all the force I could muster. As my forearms hit my hips, my body mass forced them apart, splitting the zip ties. Thank God for marine combat training. Before dark-hair realized what had happened, I swiveled, grabbed his gun hand, and used it to strike him hard in his left eye. He took a step back as I wrenched the weapon from his grip.

At the same moment, the first gunshots cracked. The man who had previously been holding Kaitlin collapsed in a bloody heap. Blondie was quickest to react. Sensing what had happened behind him, he swung a high kick, arcing in a ninety-degree turn. His boot collected my face before I could raise my gun, sending me to the ground.

Dusit, who had been following, stomped my face into the dirt as he climbed over me to board the plane.

More shots rang out. The SUVs still hadn't crossed the full distance between the edge of the strip and where the plane stood. I didn't know who they were, but I was glad as all hell that they'd arrived. The crack of gunfire repeated, a round taking out the rear screen of the gray SUV that had brought Kaitlin. The car didn't move, and no one got out of it. Another thug down. A third shot put a hole in the plane's fuselage just behind Alroy.

He screamed at blondie as he climbed on board, "Just get in, leave Sharp here, he doesn't matter now."

The plane's engines revved harder. Alroy held a hand out for blondie. Just as he attempted to pull him up, I lunged for the thug's feet and yanked his body back out of the doorway. He turned on me like a man possessed, punching hard into my head with his right hand while his left clung desperately to Alroy's wrist.

Alroy didn't wait, yelling to the pilot, "Go, go!"

The plane edged forward. Although the gun had slipped from my hand in the onslaught, at least I had the wherewithal to lower my head to minimize blondie's blows. When he hesitated for a second, I raised my left hand and brought it down in a powerful chop on his wrist. With a total lack of elegance, I followed through by grabbing a handful of his hair, yanking his head backward. He fought for grip on the bottom lip of the doorway before sliding down and smashing his skull on the dirt runway. It wasn't a knockout blow, but the moment the plane's rear wheel ran over his face was.

I leaped forward toward the plane's door, but it wasn't there. The aircraft's engines revved louder than ever, as it rolled across the dirt. I jumped to the left, wrapping my fingers around the side edge of the disappearing opening. The plane pulled me along, my feet dragging through the dust. I scraped and pulled until half of my body made it inside. I thought I had a chance. Then I didn't.

A force of nature thudded into my back and dragged me out through the opening. Dark-hair. Once again clinging onto the rim of the door, I kicked at his head, left foot, then right, attempting to use my heel as a sap. The thug wore the blows, slowly clambering up my body until his arms stretched around my waist. Each foot the plane moved forward brought greater resistance, making it almost impossible to hold on. Abruptly the plane slammed into a pothole on the runway, causing my right hand to lose its grip. A second away from falling.

In a last-ditch attempt, I clenched my left hand to maintain what hold I had, while digging in with my right elbow to jab at dark-hair's head. I felt my elbow connect with the side of his face, snapping his head back, but the blow caused the fingers on my left hand to slip. I'd lost precious leverage in my fight to stay with the plane.

The sound of another gunshot resonated above the engine noise. In an instant, dark-hair released his hold and fell away. I half heaved, half jumped back onto the cabin floor. I struggled forward on my belly, grasping at the bolted-in passenger seat legs somewhere in front of me. Contact. I closed my fist around the metal and hauled myself fully on board.

I'd never fought so hard to get on a plane I'd sworn not to board. Situations change.

Halfway down the strip now, and the aircraft's speed picked up noticeably. I glanced up to see Alroy seated behind the pilot with Sanit across the aisle from him. Kaitlin sat in the seat at the rear of her. The detective's gun arced between the two of them.

Where was Dusit?

A heavy boot thundered into my face. I slid backward, back out of the aircraft, my feet smashing onto the runway, the ground tearing at my toes. For the third time in the space of a minute, I clung desperately to the edge of the opening. Craning upward, through a curtain of blood, I saw Dusit. Poised with his fingers wrapped firmly around the parachutists' safety rail above the door, he'd swung around from the rear of the craft to blindside me. He retracted both feet for a final assault.

A second blow would send me spinning off the aircraft. As his boots swung toward me, I stretched my left hand upward, again casting for a seat leg. Nothing. In one irrevocable act, I relinquished all grip on anything attached to the plane. I lunged forward while rolling to the right. As Dusit's feet swept past me at the bottom point of his swing, I wrapped my arms around his ankles. With the surprise addition of my weight, he lost his hold on the safety bar, his back smashing onto the aircraft floor. He slipped toward the doorway, grasping wildly for the seat leg I'd aimed for earlier. He must have found it because his progress out the door halted. Dusit's lower legs now hung out the aircraft door with me hanging off them. I frantically reached upward, my left hand finding his leather belt. That was all I needed. In one swift motion, I hauled myself up, clenched my right fist, and smashed him hard on his cheek. He responded by clenching his left arm around my neck to steady himself. I hit him hard in the gut. He grunted as he curled forward in reaction to the blow. In doing so, his grip on the seat leg failed. My mistake. We both resumed the slide. Our bodies wrestled desperately in some sort of no-man's-land, half in and half out of the plane. The stream of wind funneling down the side of the fuselage acted as a suction, pulling us further out the opening. Dusit wriggled, fighting for something to hold on to. We slipped further; I clawed for the edge of the door, but my fingers had become sweaty and had trouble gripping. Dust and grit streamed from the rubber tires as they pounded the earth, attempting to break free of the ground. I could barely see as it matted the blood into my eyes. One last attempt to clasp the doorway, find some purchase.

232

Suddenly my fingers found the edge and held it.

The plane's nose tilted upward.

At that precise moment, the aircraft thumped back down for its final contact with the runway. The sharp movement jolted me sideways and backward, the metal rim of the doorway slipping from my grip. Flailing miserably, Dusit and I rolled awkwardly out of the plane, through the air, and back onto the hard gravel surface that was moving way too fast.

Chapter 42

Disoriented, partially blinded by the blood that had congealed in my eyes, but still conscious, my first reaction was to rise and deal with Dusit. I failed completely. Three seconds of the world spinning and I collapsed into the same messy heap that had fallen from the plane. Trying for a second attempt, I wiped the blood from my face and sat up, resting on one arm. Small steps, well no steps at all, really. It took a minute for my pupils to focus before I saw him. Eight feet away, Dusit lay comatose on the ground.

I hoped he was dead.

Every movement an exercise in agony, each breath an effort, I forced myself to stand for a second time. It was touch and go. As I stared hopelessly up into the blue sky, the Cessna arched away from the runway in a lazy circle, far out of reach. The pain that tortured my body felt inconsequential compared to the ache in my heart as I watched Michael Alroy sweep Sanit and Kaitlin off to certain death.

A mechanical rumbling sound caught my attention, I quelled my misery and looked to its source. Further down the runway, clouds of dust spouted into the air. An SUV bore straight down on where I stood. I didn't care if the vehicle contained the good guys or the bad guys. With Kaitlin and Sanit lost, I really didn't care about anything else.

The car skidded to a halt in a shroud of powdery grit. Both front doors opened. An officer in LAPD uniform got out of the driver's side. Samuel Chen climbed out of the passenger seat, his arm wrapped in a sling. Then, before I uttered a word, a voice boomed out of the dust behind the driver.

"Nicholas, you look like shit."

Part of me felt relieved to see the big fella, but another part cowered at the thought of breaking the news about Kaitlin and Sanit being on board that plane.

"Are you all right?" he asked.

"Jack, they're gone."

"Who's gone?"

"Kaitlin and Sanit, they're both on that Cessna. Alroy has them. You've probably figured that out by now, it was Alroy."

He nodded.

"Alroy is going to return Sanit to her homeland before arranging her murder," I said as I collapsed back onto the dirt.

"Shit. What about Kaitlin?" he asked. His voice trembled.

I stared up at the sky. The pilot had just about completed his arc, about to return to his previous incoming course. I barely found the strength to speak.

"Jack, Kaitlin won't be on that plane when it lands."

The big fella collapsed onto one knee, his grief palatable.

Detective Chen bent down next to me. "Are you all right, Sharp?"

"Define all right." Not much of a response.

My eyes remained focused on the plane, completing its circle. Damn thing still so close, yet frustratingly out of reach. I could almost...

235

"Shit! Shit! Holy Shit!" I sprang to my feet. "Detective, is that your car?"

"Yeah, sure."

"How well is it equipped?"

"Full tactical in the locked box in the back," he replied. "Why?"

"Snipers rifle?"

"Yes, of course. I said full tactical and I'm a marksman."

I flung out my palm toward the confused man. "Key."

"To the box?"

"Hell yes."

Chen reached into his pocket but hesitated in offering me the key to his mobile armory.

I grabbed it from his hand as I brushed past him. "Jack, you drive."

Greatrex reacted at lightning speed. That's what made us a team. I looked back up at the Cessna. His loop complete, the pilot's course would take him at a ninety-degree angle, directly across the top of the runway.

We had one single, slim chance.

Greatrex sped down the runway, sending more dust spiraling into the sky. I leaned over the rear seat and unlocked Chen's armory. Good to his word, the ACU man had what we needed. Carefully packaged in custom-cut foam lay the familiar outline of a Barrett M82 rifle. Chen and the LAPD knew their guns.

Bumping down a dirt runway wasn't the optimum environment to assemble a precision rifle, but there would be no time to go through the process once we reached our destination.

"How's the gun?" asked Greatrex from the front seat.

"Barrett M82," I responded.

236

"Thank God."

I wasn't ready to thank God yet, but we'd see.

The SUV slurred left and then right as we bore down the runway. I ignored the movement.

The fifty-caliber rifle came in two parts. I pulled out the lower receiver, lowered the bipod legs, and removed the mid-lock pin. As carefully as possible, I let the bolt shield slide forward. Resting that section of the weapon beside me, I then reached down into the box and retrieved the upper receiver. It had been years since I'd fired or assembled one of these, and vital seconds were ticking by.

Greatrex pushed the vehicle harder, its engine wailing in a strained raucousness.

Despite the chaos, I had to focus on the job at hand. The big fella would have my back. I had to trust him, just as I always had. I forced Kaitlin from my thoughts. This wouldn't be the first time I had to emotionally compartmentalize. I needed to treat this like any other kill. A skewered state of mind would impact my effectiveness.

With the upper receiver in my hand, I slid the barrel forward into its firing position. I almost forgot to remove the rubber battery bumper before I placed the receiver against my stomach and pulled the spring-loaded lock into place.

I glanced up; we looked to be about two hundred yards from the end of the runway, Greatrex would have to slow soon. What I had in mind couldn't be done if the car arrived amidst a swirl of thick dust.

I hoisted the lower part of the gun over the seat and slid the upper section into place. The back of the vehicle swayed from side to side as Jack braked. I inserted the rear and mid lock pins. It took a couple of attempts, but I managed.

The car had almost stopped by the time I inserted the telescopic sight. The final piece in the puzzle: reach back into the box, grab the magazine assembly and push it into place. Click and complete. The entire process hadn't taken much time, but we didn't have much time.

As the SUV rolled to a halt, I leaped out, rifle in hand. Everything now depended on the position of the aircraft. I looked skyward. The Cessna had straightened up but was yet to cross the end of the runway. Nose pointing high, the plane climbed. It was difficult to be certain from the ground, but I estimated their altitude to be somewhere between four and six thousand feet. The Barrett had an accurate range of over nineteen hundred yards, fifty-seven hundred feet, so maybe I had a shot... literally.

There would be seconds in this. I ran to the front of the SUV and placed the rifle on the hood, placing the legs on the edge closest to me. By getting down on one knee, and using the bipod, I angled the barrel high enough to allow the plane into the scope's view.

I gradually grew aware of a commotion in the distance as Chen's crew moved to catch up with us. Again, I knew Greatrex would take care of them, leaving me to do my job. I needed to focus.

A second later, I had the Cessna in my sights. Firing into the engine to bring the plane down would be pointless, it would only end the two women's lives sooner. My target was more specific. I made several split-second judgments about distance, wind velocity, and the all-important slipstream coming off the aircraft's fuselage. There would also be some backdraft from the plane's propeller. One miscalculation would mean certain disaster for everyone on board.

As was my way, I slowed my breathing and steadied my hands. I always fired after exhaling, in the moment of pause before inhaling again. The rhythm of my respiratory cycle had to be even and smooth, like waves.

In my mind, I pictured the layout of the interior of the aircraft as I'd briefly glimpsed it. Alroy perched behind the pilot, Sanit across the aisle, and Kaitlin in the seat behind her. If any of them had swapped positions, this would be all over, and not in a good way. The plane currently presented with its starboard side toward my position. That was vital. There would have been no plan at all if it headed in the opposite direction. There was barely a plan now.

The aircraft moved fast, its heading a little less than ninety degrees– almost perpendicular to the runway. I had only a few seconds of opportunity, one shot at best.

Through the scope, I saw the Cessna bounce slightly as it hit some turbulence. Enough movement to kill my opportunity. I inhaled again. Thoughts of Kaitlin crept into my head, our history together. Rookie mistake, I pushed her from my mind.

Focused, cold, professional, detached. That's what she needed from me at this moment.

I took another breath and surveyed my prey through the scope. The real world. The plane had stopped bouncing. I adjusted my aim for the fuselage, under the window directly behind the pilot. Shooting through glass involved more variables. There were enough of those already, and the fuselage was thin. I needed to go for a body shot, mid-torso. In normal conditions, that would be the safe shot. These conditions would be as far from normal as you could get.

The aircraft bounced again, higher, I paused, figuring I had less than five seconds left before my target flew out of range.

I followed its progress with the point of the barrel. Suddenly the plane found smooth air, I'd reached the end of a breath, three seconds left, finger resting on the trigger.

Had the wind picked up?

Two seconds.

Squeeze.

The crack echoed down the valley.

Normally a shooter can see the result of his or her shot immediately. I saw nothing. The Cessna didn't falter in its flight path, but that didn't mean anything yet. I was certain I'd hit the plane, but I doubted the pinpoint accuracy of the shot. It was always an impossible ask.

Greatrex stood next to me. More of Chen's people arrived. Damn it all. The aircraft continued to fly southeast toward Mexico, and I could do nothing more to stop it. Kaitlin and Sanit would die. I looked to Greatrex, floundering for words.

"I've failed, I've failed both of them." The big fella gazed at me with a look of compassion that only one old friend could offer another when there was nothing more they could do to help. Our eyes locked in despair.

Chen arrived beside me. "Give me the gun."

"What?" I asked.

"Sharp, give me the damn gun."

I passed it over. He held up the weapon with his good arm, pointing it at the aircraft.

"It's too late, Chen, they're out of range," I mumbled.

"I know that," he replied, but look man, there's some movement.

We all stared upward. Chen was right. The Cessna bounced around erratically, sometimes slipping sideways. The aircraft's reaction to the turbulence that I'd noted earlier had been steadier, more controlled. The three of us held our breath, not only willing the aircraft not to fall out of the sky but also praying it would turn.

More wobbles. The plane began a sharp dive. I inhaled involuntarily. A moment later, the nose leveled out. Breathe again. One prayed answered, one to go. Suddenly the right-wing dipped down. This time, the movement didn't appear to be a wild lunge; it was a smoother transition, more deliberate. Slowly, the Cessna's route formed a different arc. As the aircraft gradually straightened out, its new flight path became clear.

The plane now headed toward the airfield it had just abandoned... toward us.

As the Cessna's wheels touched the dirt, kicking up a curtain of dust, the relief was immense. Once it had completed its landing, the aircraft swung around and headed toward where we'd regrouped near the hanger. The plane taxied to a stop right in front of us; I stepped forward to open the side door. Chen's men stepped up, guns drawn, mostly pointing at the pilot who immediately shut down the engines and raised his hands in the air. A couple more ACU people stood behind me, weapons raised, but I didn't wait for them.

The door slid open, and I stuck my head inside. Not necessarily a smart move, but I was beyond caring. On the right of the cabin, behind the pilot, Detective Michael Alroy lay prone across his seat, held there by his seatbelt, his shirt soaked in a liquid swathe of crimson blood. A fifty-caliber round will do that to you.

Opposite Alroy, Sanit sat strapped to her seat. Blood splatter covered her clothes, her hair, and much of her face. She stared down at Alroy. The defeated face of evil.

Behind Sanit, perched Kaitlin Reed. She wasn't strapped in but had wedged herself back into her seat by placing a knee on the rear of Sanit's seat and a foot on the seat across the aisle. Her wrists remained bound, but they now held a gun. Michael Alroy's gun. Kaitlin's arms stretched forward. If you didn't know her hands were tied, you'd be forgiven for thinking it was some form of the shooter's stance.

Kaitlin's weapon pointed across the cabin, directly at the rear of the pilot's head.

"Kaitlin, are you alright?" I asked.

As Chen's men took control of the pilot, she lowered the gun, turned to me, and smiled.

"Never better."

Epilogue

The warm surge of applause underscored the cries of heartfelt support. A tide of emotion. Over a thousand faces looked expectantly up at the stage. It wasn't Woodstock, but when word traveled that this would be Kha Cring's return US performance, people had flocked to this small community festival.

Kha Cring was a smaller ensemble now. Dusit Salae was firmly seconded in US custody, several agencies fighting over the right to prosecute him. Detective Chen assured us he'd been cooperating with authorities, giving up more duplicitous contacts within Homeland Security than Chen had even suspected. Still, Dusit's sentence would be a long one.

Sanit enlisted the help of some extra musicians for this performance. I'd been delighted to offer my services on keyboards and guitar. My old friend, Barry Flannigan, generously agreed to fill in on bass for Sonny, Kha Cring's fallen bass player.

My heart warmed as I looked across the stage to the band's drummer. An astute observer would note the occasional expression of discomfort as he reached across his toms to execute a drum roll, but Ram's face told a story of determination outweighing pain. Sanit and I had been stunned when, back at the abandoned airfield, Chen told us that Ram was still alive, and that the detective's medical team believed he should survive his wounds. For the first time in many months, Sanit's tears had been of joy.

Sanit began the second song. She strummed her guitar with force and confidence, reminiscent of a young Joni Mitchell. As her voice enveloped the space, she mustered a depth of emotional conviction that few artists could access. There were times during the song that I needed to remind myself to keep playing, rather than stop and listen. Such was her spell.

A final chord, Sanit began to speak. The noise from the crowd retreated to a whisper.

"With all my heart, I thank you all for coming tonight. You'll have read the news, heard about our adventures through the media, you know our journey to this point has not been an easy one."

A sea of faces stared up at the singer, hanging off every word.

"Our younger selves took up music because we loved it, we loved playing together, and in time we discovered our music held value for other people. Your response over many years has brought us great joy. Sadly, our music has also ushered in moments of deep despair. None of us ever considered the unimaginable price that some in our group would have to pay for the privilege of being musicians of principle."

Sanit looked around, her eyes making contact with each band member. While she offered a nod in my direction, Ram received an unbridled gaze of adoration as a grin permeated both their faces.

"It goes without saying that tonight's performance, and every show we do from here on, will be dedicated to the memories of Sonny, Kamon and Chaiya. Many of you won't remember Chaiya, he was with us early on, but like Sonny and Kamon, he sacrificed his life for the freedoms our countrymen and women have so far been denied."

Ram bowed his head, staring down at his drum kit, I wondered where his thoughts had taken him. Sanit stood upright and proud, facing down the crowd and the world.

"I will not speak for long, but I tell you this. For the rest of our lives, or until our government wields its power for the good of our people, Kha Cring will stand loudly and proudly for the cause of freedom and democracy. The tyrants can go to hell!"

As she raised one hand, her fist clenched in a powerful salute, Sanit smiled at the erupting ocean of humanity. For two minutes, squeals and hollers resonated across the field in a show of love and support. The cacophony would have continued longer if Sanit hadn't turned back to Ram and nodded.

Ram stood up, at least three spotlights highlighting his enormous presence. He looked deep into the crowd while holding both hands high, a drumstick in each. His jaw jutted forward, his mouth clenched in resolve. He suddenly emitted an almighty roar. Driven by forces beyond this world, he slammed his sticks down onto the drum skins in a thunderous explosion, releasing a pulsating, primal rhythm into the darkness.

Kha Cring's war cry raged upward to the heavens.

"Nicholas, are you all right?"

Kaitlin's concern was appreciated, but I didn't do well at this sort of thing. As we strolled along the Venice boardwalk, the jugglers and the skaters became a welcome distraction.

"Nicholas." Damn, she wasn't letting this go.

The Pacific sunset was warm, but it struggled to diffuse the unsettled state I found myself wallowing in.

That morning, the day after the concert, we'd all sat down with Samuel Chen. As we reviewed the deceitful web that Michael Alroy had spun, it became clear that the repercussions would be far-reaching. It was important for Sanit and Ram to hear the lengths that Alroy had gone to, setting up Chen and his team as the fall guys, manipulating me, not to mention deceiving a bag full of federal and state agencies. I'd apologized to Chen for assuming his guilt. His reaction was to the point.

"We were all victims of that man's greed, Sharp. It's pointless for you to assume all the blame."

In my head, I knew he was right, but for someone who'd built two careers around using his head, my sense of logic didn't always land in the right place.

The remaining members of Kha Cring also needed to know the results of the investigation. Chen told us their homeland's government forces had backed off completely. In a bid to reduce his own sentence, Dusit Salae provided so much information about his government's subversive ways, that those in charge realized they'd done their own cause more harm than good. Kha Cring had been removed from their hit list, permanently.

Sanit and Ram would stay in LA for now, and as we'd seen the night before, their course remained unchanged, their voices undiminished.

All positive outcomes.

Then I'd spent the afternoon with Tommy Dabbs' mother.

"Nicholas?"

Kailin's blond hair fell across her cheek; the casualness of her beauty had always beguiled me. Because of her looks, many people underestimated the character and determination that she held within. I was not one of them. I was certain the pilot of the Cessna was not one of them either.

My eyes followed a young skateboarder, risking life and limb as he weaved in and out of the pedestrians. When that distraction ran out, I studied the footpath as though it held the meaning of life, I wasn't being particularly grown-up about this. Time had taught me that I found it easier to face down villains with automatic weapons rather than my own emotional baggage.

I raised my head.

"Kaitlin, this is complicated." So now I sounded like a rom-com... for God's sake.

I tried again. "When I ask a favor, my friends, my good friends, come running. You stepped up without question, and it nearly cost you your life. Jack chips in and finds himself in constant peril over and over again. And of course..."

"Tommy Dabbs," said Kaitlin.

I swallowed hard. "Yes, Tommy. He fought his way out of a desperate world and built a life for himself. Then I ask him a favor, knowing he'd say yes, knowing he'd follow you anywhere."

I paused. The words were there, I just needed to find them.

"Tommy is dead because I called on him," I said.

Kaitlin looked at me, her eyes glowing with warmth, understanding. "Nicholas, Tommy died because he was killed by extremely bad men led by someone even worse."

"At my behest," I responded.

"Nicholas, can you get this into your overly stubborn head? Jack, me, Tommy, even the general, come to you because you're a good man. You care, you protect people. We want to be part

247

of that."

I sensed my own withdrawal from the conversation. Discomfort.

"Kaitlin, I'm also a dangerous man to be around."

She looked me in the eye. Never one to cater for self-pity.

"How many people are alive now because of you?"

I gazed out across the beach toward the ocean, then back to the boardwalk. Anywhere but Kaitlin's eyes. A pathetic attempt at escape.

"Yes Nicholas, you are a dangerous man, but that's not always a bad thing. You're just going to have to get over yourself, get used to who you are, and enjoy the ride."

Nicholas Sharp, rider on a storm.

Afterword

Get your FREE electronic copy of the NICHOLAS SHARP origins Novella PLAY OUT, the latest news about new releases and some other exciting freebies along the way by joining my mailing list at my website: https://markmannock.com

Although you can begin reading the **NICHOLAS SHARP** thriller series at any point here is my suggested order of reading:

1. **KILLSONG** (NS thriller No. 1-*available on Amazon*)
2. **BLOOD NOTE** (A NS short story-*available exclusively to my mailing list members. I'll send you the link 7 days after sign-up*)
3. **LETHAL SCORE** (NS thriller No. 2-*available on Amazon*)
4. **HELL'S CHOIR** (NS thriller No. 3-*available on Amazon*)
5. **SILENT VOICE** (NS thriller No. 4-available on Amazon)
6. **COUNTERPOINT** (NS thriller No. 5-available on Amazon)
7. **ECHO BLUE** (NS thriller No. 6, pre-order on Amazon, out August 2023)

PLAY OUT-an origins novella (*available exclusively to my mailing list members on sign-up*) can be read at any point. The story takes you back to when Nicholas Sharp left the U.S. Marines.

<u>**Reviews are life's blood to an author**</u>.

If you've enjoyed the **Nicholas Sharp** thrillers please consider leaving a review on the book's Amazon page.

What readers are saying about the Nicholas Sharp Series:

"I had to keep reading to the end, could not put it away until I had finished."

"I love Lee Child and now have another author who is just as good."

"Jack Reacher's attitude... John Lennon's sensibilities."

"I really enjoyed the sniper-musician-reluctant warrior character..."

"I've read hundreds of books throughout the years and the pandemic has provided me with extra time to discover more reading treasures. Play Out (Nicholas Sharp Origins novella) is one of the best."

"Without a doubt this is a cracking novel... the story then keeps at you in leaps and bounds! Full of action all the way. Just brilliant!"

Acknowledgements

My heartfelt thanks and love to Sarah, Anisha and Jack for your love, tolerance and support. Lachlan, your counsel and wisdom is eternally appreciated.

Cover by Anisha Mannock

About the Author

Mark Mannock was born in Melbourne, Australia. He has had an extensive career in the music industry including supporting, recording with or writing for Tina Turner, Joni Mitchell, The Eurythmics, Irene Cara and David Hudson. His recorded work with Lia Scallon has twice been long-listed for Grammy Awards.

As a composer/songwriter Mark's music has been used across the world in countless television and theatre contexts, including the 'American Survivor' TV series and 'Sleuth' playwright Anthony Shaffer's later productions.

Mark has also been active in music education across Australia promoting student's ownership and voice in their own educational music journeys. He has won several awards for his endeavours in this area.

Mark is presently writing the successful 'Nicholas Sharp' thriller series about a disillusioned former US sniper whose past plagues him as he makes his way in the contemporary music industry. Sharp is a man whose insatiable curiosity and embedded moral compass lead him to places he ought not go. The series is currently read in over 50 countries.

Mark lives in Kettering, Tasmania with his family. His travels around the globe act as inspirations for his writing.

Mark enjoys hearing from his readers, so please feel free to contact him.

What readers are saying about the Nicholas Sharp Series:

"I had to keep reading to the end, could not put it away until I had finished."

"I love Lee Child and now have another author who is just as good."

"Jack Reacher's attitude... John Lennon's sensibilities."

"I really enjoyed the sniper-musician-reluctant warrior character..."

"I've read hundreds of books throughout the years and the pandemic has provided me with extra time to discover more reading treasures. Play Out (Nicholas Sharp Origins novella) is one of the best."

"Without a doubt this is a cracking novel... the story then keeps at you in leaps and bounds! Full of action all the way. Just brilliant!"

You can connect with me on:

🌐 https://markmannock.com

📘 https://www.facebook.com/markmannockbooks

Subscribe to my newsletter:

✉ https://markmannock.com

Also by Mark Mannock

PLAY OUT
A Terrorist attack on the London Underground. Nicholas Sharp doesn't think so.

While on leave from Iraq, the U.S. Marine Sniper finds himself intervening when innocent lives are threatened. He walks away, but for Sharp, it's never that easy. Something doesn't feel right. Twenty-four hours later, everything is wrong.

The brief solace he finds in his beloved piano is shattered when Sharp becomes the attacker's next target. Step up or step away. Nicholas Sharp doesn't like to kill, but he sure as hell knows how to.

Somewhere between Tom Clancy's *Jack Ryan* and Robert Crais' *Elvis Cole*, Nicholas Sharp may be a flawed hero, but you certainly want him on your side.

"I've read hundreds of books throughout the years and the pandemic has provided me with extra time to discover more reading treasures. Play Out is one of the best." **Goodreads Reviewer-5 STARS**

The Nicholas Sharp origins novella PLAY OUT is sent to you FREE when you join my mailing list at https://markmannock.com

COUNTERPOINT
Nicholas Sharp Thriller #5

Looking in the mirror, he saw only death...

Pursued by one of the world's most efficient and ruthless assassins, Nicholas Sharp almost admires the deadly operator's meticulous talents, until the assassin starts coming after Sharp through his friends. Sharp's investigations reveal that the killer also has another target in sight: the US Secretary of Defense. Is there a dark connection?

Face to face with a past he'd considered banished from his memory, Nicholas Sharp questions not only his own moral compass but also his slim chance of survival.

Available on Amazon:

http://www.amazon.com/dp/B0BVTVWZ6N
http://www.amazon.co.uk/dp/B0BVTVWZ6N
http://www.amazon.com.au/dp/B0BVTVWZ6N
https://www.amazon.ca/dp/B0BVTVWZ6N

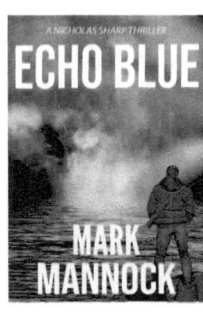

ECHO BLUE
Nicholas Sharp Thriller #6

Are you safe?...

Nicholas Sharp receives a mysterious phone call from Jack Greatrex... then Greatrex disappears.

In a hunt that takes him through South America, Texas, the mountains of Northern Spain and eventually the Middle East, Sharp encounters world renowned environmental activist Dr Deagan Jones from the notorious Crimson Wave. As Sharp uncovers a chain of complex deceptions, Jones' teenage son is kidnapped. The stakes never higher, the ex-Marine sniper turned musician fights to prevent an environmental and humanitarian catastrophe with unimaginable consequences.

Available on Amazon:

http://www.amazon.com/dp/B0BVV25R2F
http://www.amazon.co.uk/dp/B0BVV25R2F
http://www.amazon.com.au/dp/B0BVV25R2F
https://www.amazon.ca/dp/B0BVV25R2F

KILLSONG

Nicholas Sharp Thriller #1

Nicholas Sharp is a killer musician... literally!
Turning his back on the military system that turned him into a murderer when he shot an innocent man, Sharp is grateful to have found refuge in a career as a successful musician. But while he is preparing to back well-known former rock star Robbie West on a USO tour of Iraq, a close friend and her daughter disappear.

In a deadly game of cat and mouse across three continents, Sharp discovers there's more at stake than his own life and those close to him. As relentless shadows from his past chase him down, he faces a brutal choice. Kill or be killed.

"I had to keep reading to the end, could not put it away until I had finished." **Amazon Reader- 5 STARS**

"Jack Reachers attitude... John Lennon's sensibilities." **Goodreads Reviewer- 5 STARS**

Available on Amazon:
  http://www.amazon.com/dp/B08CT1FHF5
  http://www.amazon.co.uk/dp/B08CT1FHF5
  http://www.amazon.com.au/dp/B08CT1FHF5
  https://www.amazon.ca/dp/B08CT1FHF5

LETHAL SCORE
Nicholas Sharp Thriller #2

"A great book that has more twists and turns than you can imagine. Pick up and read at all costs." **Goodreads Reviewer 5 STARS**

You can't stop someone with nothing to lose...

Nicholas Sharp is on a tour through Europe, the concerts are sold out and the former Marine sniper turned musician is living in luxury thanks to promoter Antonio Ascardi.

Suddenly it all goes wrong. People are dying along the way and Sharp is blamed. Now a hunted man, accused of terrorist crimes across the continent, Nicholas Sharp must fight for his life and freedom.

Available on Amazon:
   http://www.amazon.com/dp/B08CSYKG18
   http://www.amazon.co.uk/dp/B08CSYKG18
   http://www.amazon.com.au/dp/B08CSYKG18
   https://www.amazon.ca/dp/B08CSYKG18

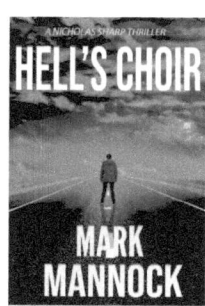

HELL'S CHOIR
Nicholas Sharp Thriller #3

A goodwill visit to Sudan, what could possibly go wrong?

Nicholas Sharp is performing as part of a political and cultural group representing the US. Suddenly caught up in the middle of a political coup, the leader of the American contingent goes missing and his security staff murdered.

Communication with the outside world is cut off. It falls to Sharp and Greatrex to track their missing leader down.

But then things get really complicated…

"The story then keeps at you in leaps and bounds! Full of action all the way. Just brilliant!" **Amazon Reader-5 STARS**

"Great read and a fun ride." **Amazon Reader-5 STARS**

Available on Amazon:
http://www.amazon.com/dp/B08LRB8CWN
http://www.amazon.co.uk/dp/B08LRB8CWN
http://www.amazon.com.au/dp/B08LRB8CWN
https://www.amazon.ca/dp/B08LRB8CWN

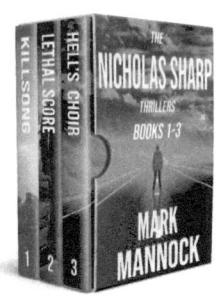

The NICHOLAS SHARP THRILLERS BOOKS 1-3 BOXSET

KILLSONG
LETHAL SCORE
HELL'S CHOIR
Three great Nicholas Sharp Novels in one Box Set

http://www.amazon.com/dp/B08NYLGW1G
http://www.amazon.co.uk/dp/B08NYLGW1G
http://www.amazon.com.au/dp/B08NYLGW1G
https://www.amazon.ca/dp/B08NYLGW1G

BLOOD NOTE
A Short Story Prequel to the Thriller
KILLSONG *(should be read after KILLSONG-available FREE to mailing list subscribers 7 days after sign-up)*

Just turn around and walk away. That was all Nicholas Sharp had to do when the mysterious and intoxicating Elena approached him for help.

She knew far too much about him. The warning signs were all there.

Sharp didn't listen to them.

What followed for the former Marine Sniper turned musician, was a harrowing night of violence, deceit and intrigue.

When the sunrise ushered in a new day, Sharp thought it was all over...but it was really just beginning.

https://markmannock.com